LUCKY UNIVERSE

LUCKY'S MARINES | BOOK ONE

JOSHUA JAMES

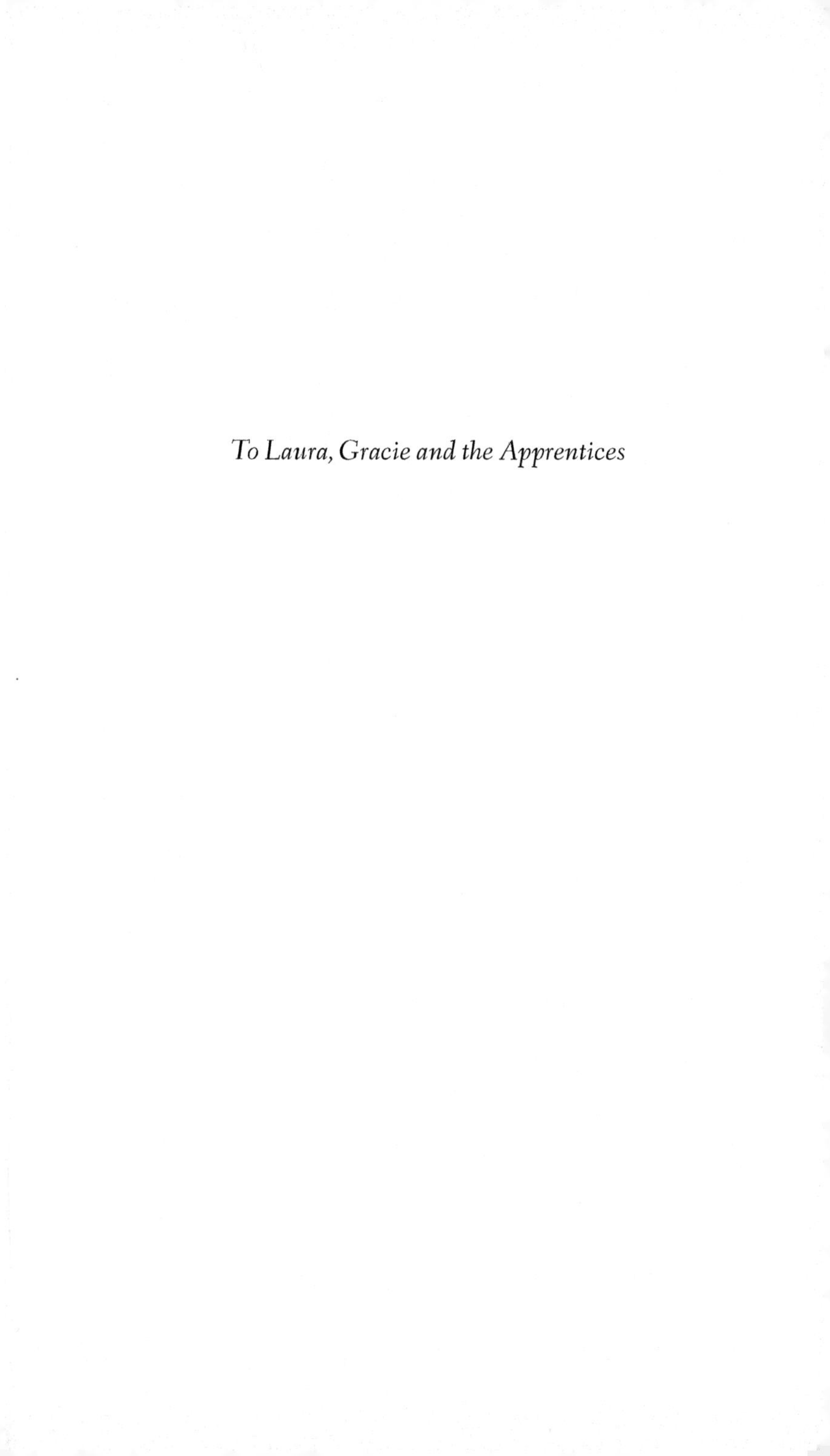

To Laura, Gracie and the Apprentices

Sign up for the author's Reader Crew and get a free copy of the prequel story LUCKY SHOT. You won't believe what Lucky was like before he was lucky.

www.LuckyShotBook.com

PROLOGUE

"I SEE YOU!" screamed Skunk from the turret above as the ancient pulse pounder belched a volley of ionized slugs in rapid succession. "C'mon now, get some!"

A steady stream of used thermal cartridges tumbled into the cramped cabin of the skimmer.

The old ground hugger bounced and bucked from the recoil of the giant cannon as the hover engine struggled gamely to keep it afloat. Up front the driver swore in some language only he knew.

Nobody on this rock was from this rock.

Jolly sure as hell wasn't, and right now he was seriously considering his life choices.

He leapt up and swung his pulse rifle into the firing port on his side of the skimmer. The two screw-ups next to him did the opposite, both ducking their heads in unison.

Considering they were stoned, Jolly was surprised they'd reacted at all. He wished he was stoned right now.

Up top, Skunk was still firing orgasmically.

Jolly peered down the cracked scope of his worn out rifle. It was second-hand garbage, just like everything else he had. An ancient heads-up display projected into his mind. His embedded AI was off-the-shelf, but beggars can't be choosers.

An image from the skimmer's big battle drone floating somewhere overhead formed in his mind. He couldn't control it, but he could plug into it, and could probably get a second view from one of the tiny grasshopper drones making periodic sweeps. But he didn't need it.

He spotted two miners running away from the remnants of an old rover engulfed in a cloud of kicked-up dirt and rock. It was one of the company rovers, indistinguishable from any of the other ubiquitous shit-colored gear here.

At least two bodies were mashed into the twisted mess of the shredded rover.

Jolly sighted on the closest of the fleeing pair and squeezed off a pulse just as the skimmer bucked. In a blink, the running miners disappeared, replaced by huge steaming divots in the dirt.

"Those were mine, asshole!" Jolly screamed up at the turret.

Skunk was just a selfish bitch with a cannon.

"Private Skunk!" exploded the snarling voice of Sarge from the front of the skimmer.

The shooting stopped.

"Yeah, boss?" came Skunk's innocent reply.

"What the hell are you firing at?"

"Saw a disturbance, sir. Had to act fast," he said, unconvincingly.

He popped his head down from the turret, ear flaps hanging halfway to the steel grated floor. "Probably saved our lives."

Sarge sighed. "Jolly?"

"Definitely looked like they were up to something," he lied, aware Sarge knew he hadn't seen a damn thing.

Sarge sighed again. "File a report when we get back. Again."

Paperwork was the company's latest attempt to rein them in and save the lives of a few miners in the process. Jolly had to admit it kinda worked. He even broke up a bar fight last week without killing anyone.

Maiming was more fun anyway.

Skunk's smile evaporated. "Aw, Sarge, c'mon man."

Sarge wasn't really a sergeant, of course. And Skunk wasn't a private. Jolly didn't know their real names, and didn't care. Soldiers always talked about dying for the guy next to them. Jolly wouldn't get off the shitter for anyone in this crew.

But Sarge was the boss. The mining company gave them the titles and set the hierarchy. On their paychecks it said only *security detail.*

To be honest, even that was a stretch. To quote the company's certified headshrinker, they were "mostly a group of armed lunatics with nothing to do on a small planet full of migrant miners who never really did anything at all, and definitely nothing worthy of a full security detail."

A short time after that report was filed, the shrink died in a small arms accident at the shooting range behind the security hut. Tragic.

But the company paid on time, and in the mighty Union of Merchant Settlements, that was almost unheard of. Jolly heard the Union wasn't even paying real soldiers anymore, but they heard lots of strange things these days, particularly about the military. Especially about the home world. Jolly was starting to believe it wasn't just gossip.

As if to prove his point the man in combat armor sitting next to Sarge put his hand firmly on Sarge's shoulder.

This creep was military. Union Marine. The genuine article.

He'd shown up this morning at the security trailer wearing his shiny black armor and flanked by fifty Union soldiers. Faster than you could take a piss, they were suiting up and jumping in the skimmers and heading out to ... well, somewhere. That was *need to know*. Or something.

The soldiers were behind them in the other three skimmers.

That's us, thought Jolly. Private security. Tip of the spear.

"We need to hurry," the creep said in a monotone voice that was absolutely not hurried at all. "Let your men do as they please."

Sarge looked at the meaty hand on his shoulder, then nodded. He looked back at Skunk.

"Just ... go easy," he said, as the hand slid slowly off his shoulder.

Skunk blew him a kiss and pulled himself back up into the turret.

It was the creep's eyes, Jolly decided. They were just completely dead. Unreadable. It was unnerving as hell.

Gnarly kicked Jolly in the shin. The stoned asshole was still on the floor of the skimmer, his helmet bouncing against the grating. His buddy Dash was next to him, a guy who's life mission appeared to include following Gnarly around and agreeing with everything he said.

Jolly sighed, and bent over, his own helmet falling off. He hadn't bothered to clip it, and watched distractedly as it rolled to the far end of the skimmer.

"What, Gnarles?"

"Those guys," he said, waving in the direction of the creep. "They're everywhere on the home world. My sister told me. Well, her friend told her. But still. Like, everywhere. Like, they're starting to run security for, like, the City of Light."

The City of Light was the capital. It was a great name, since there was no light and barely any city.

"Security," Dash squealed. "Like us!" He laughed out loud, then realized the creep was looking straight at him so he tried to pass it off as a cough.

A moment later Jolly felt the skimmer shudder as it passed over a ridge.

Skunk let loose a string of obscenities and popped his head back down from the turret. He looked like he was in shock.

"Sarge, are you seeing this?"

Sarge was staring out the skimmer's front window. He didn't say anything, but his broad shoulders suddenly slumped.

The driver swore again in his peculiar tongue.

"We're here," announced the creep.

The skimmer juddered to a sudden stop.

With the engines off and the rattling floor finally still, the silence almost hurt his ears.

"That ... can't be," Sarge whispered, his voice faltering. "Can't be."

Jolly turned and looked out his firing port. It took a moment to understand what he was seeing.

A mountain? Out here?

No way.

Mountains don't just appear. Not nestled in the base of craters.

But it wasn't a mountain. The angles were too perfect. It was artificial.

It was some kind of structure covered in grey ore, as if it had been sitting in a huge cave for centuries collecting mineral deposits. Yet the shape was unmistakable once you saw it.

It was a starship.

A massive starship.

It was way bigger than the Union freighters his mother used to fly between the inner worlds. Way, way bigger than the military transports that flew to this godforsaken rock. There were huge symbols on it, visible even at this distance. Alien symbols.

Jolly felt a tingle of excitement. He had seen pictures of alien artifacts before, but he never imagined he'd actually get to see one with his own eyes. Sure, maybe if you were born in the Empire or the Alliance or the Cardinal Order this wouldn't be such a big deal. They dug them up all the time. Even the Asiatic Rings had found them.

But out here in the Union? On the edge of the void? Never.

The doors to the other skimmers were already open and soldiers were streaming out. Their lines were ragged, but they were being shepherded along at pace and with purpose by commanders in their ranks.

A cluster of weaponized drones took up positions to support the advancing group.

As the hatch to their own skimmer popped open, the creep stepped out and strode toward the alien ship as if it was something he did every day.

Jolly looked around. "What the actual hell is going on?"

No one spoke.

"Should we follow him?" asked Gnarly, pointing after

the creep. He was still sitting on the floor of the skimmer, oblivious to what the others had seen.

"I'm gonna go with a big fat *no*," Skunk replied as he dropped down from the turret.

"What do you mean, no?" Jolly realized he was talking too loud and too fast. "It's a spaceship. An *alien* spaceship!"

Skunk nodded. "Yeah, and...?"

"And, let's go check it out."

Skunk shook his head. "You think these apes are gonna be cool with us being here?" This last question was aimed at Sarge.

"Hey guys," Gnarly said.

Everyone ignored him.

"We were ordered out here," Sarge said. "What can they say?"

"I'm more concerned with what they'll do."

"Guys," Gnarly repeated.

Jolly turned to him. "What?"

Gnarly pointed. "What's that?"

The ground near the ship had started to shimmer, but before anyone could speak the sky lit up with blinding blue light as a bolt burst forth from the base of the ship.

It seemed to wash over the gathered soldiers, swirling around them like angry storm clouds.

Their drones went dead and dropped from the sky.

In unison the soldiers started messing with their head-gear, struggling almost, like they were desperate to pull off their goggles or something.

"What're they doing?" Gnarly asked.

Jolly squinted. "I can't tell," he said. "Skunk can you—"

"It looks like—" he started, then stopped.

"Holy."

"Shit."

Sarge leapt into the cockpit's jumpseat. "Get us out of here!"

"Wait, what?" said Jolly, perplexed. He didn't understand, and was suddenly jerked around as the skimmer leapt up off the ground.

They were turning, but the old rust box could only move in long, wide arcs. They swung around close to the soldiers, who turned as one.

Now Jolly could see it.

Blood poured down their faces.

They had gouged their own eyes out.

Pulpy chunks of flesh hung loose from their fingers.

"Go, go, go!" screamed Skunk.

The soldiers began marching in perfect, crisp lines heading back to the skimmers. No one stumbled or faltered.

Jolly was numb. He spotted the black combat armor of the creep that rode with them. He was near the alien ship, his cold eyes conspicuously intact.

"You are needed," he boomed in an impossibly deep voice that somehow still managed to be monotone. "Bring the others. Our time has come at last."

The creep glanced casually at their retreating skimmer, like he'd just noticed a pesky fly. He pulled out a small curved weapon of some kind. It looked like a toy.

"I'm wasting him!" Skunk yelled and leapt back into the top turret, ready for a fight.

But it was over before it started.

A blue stream of energy poured from the creep's small weapon, like water from a hose, and where it struck the skimmer it sliced straight through.

In a blink the old pulse slugger was split in half, along with the gun turret, Skunk still inside.

The split continued along the length of the skimmer,

and Sarge tried to dive out of the front cabin, but was too late. The driver screamed. The front windshield exploded and the skimmer ripped in half as its structural beams collapsed. It fell to the surface with a deafening crunch, skidding along the dirt.

Jolly was thrown around the main cabin, bouncing off the ceiling before face-planting on the grated floor.

He staggered to his feet, blood spurting from his busted nose. Dazed, he stared, mesmerized as a stream of blue light weaved lazily around him, slicing through hardened steel like a knife through potter's clay.

Gnarly slammed into him and thrust him out the open hatch just as the energy stream completed its loop and the engine core of the skimmer exploded.

Waves of scalding metal fragments screamed past Jolly's face. His eyes burned. Something sharp pinched his side.

"I'm hit—"

He rolled over to face Gnarly. A piece of metal was lodged in the middle of his face.

Jolly scrambled to his feet. His side was wet, but he couldn't feel anything. A voice told him he was in shock.

He squinted through the hot smoke billowing from the burning skimmer and found himself staring into the dead eyes of the creep. He was standing nonchalantly a hundred yards away, weapon at his side.

Jolly felt a jolt of adrenaline shoot through his body.

He jerked his pulse rifle to his shoulder as he rushed straight at the creep, screaming through the tang of salty blood on his lips.

He pumped pulse after pulse directly into the creep's central mass, as if he was shooting cans off the fence outside the security trailer.

"Come on!" he screamed, squeezing the trigger again and again.

The creep didn't even flinch, every pulse bouncing off his armor.

Jolly kept running forward, willing the rifle to do more damage, still screaming in rage. "Come on, come on, come—"

Then Jolly saw a blue light flash from the direction of the alien ship. It was just a flicker, and he ignored it, continuing to squeeze off pulses as he advanced.

And then the rifle fell from his grasp.

He looked down, dumbstruck.

His body came to a standstill, rooted in place.

He felt his meager internal tech go silent. The drone feed disappeared.

Something was chewing on him from the inside. Burrowing.

"You are needed," said a monotone voice inside his head, and he saw a hand reaching out.

He found his own arms moving in tandem with it. But he wasn't controlling them.

His callused fingers began to slowly reach toward his face, covering his eyes.

He tried to scream.

The pain was unlike anything he had ever known. He begged for it to stop, but the voice in his head was gone.

Tissue tore away, wet and sinewy. Liquid oozed down his cheek.

Jolly felt darkness engulf his mind.

And then he felt nothing.

[1]
WAKEY WAKEY

WAKE UP, Sleeping Ugly. I'm shoving all the mission specifics into your tiny little excuse for a cerebral cortex as you get this. You can access them as soon as you gain full consciousness. It's taking you longer every sleep cycle. You're getting old.

[BEGIN SITREP]

Two weeks ago

We lost communication with an outer colony of the Union. This isn't unusual, since the Union is crap at keeping their people alive. But the Empire doesn't know exactly what happened, and that *is* unusual. We have more spies in the Union than paid-off politicians.

One week ago

Communication was lost with more than one hundred Union colonies. Even by Union standards, that's a fubar situation.

Three days ago

The entire Union home world went dark. That's 3 billion sentient souls for those keeping score.

Yesterday

The Empire dropped an Occupier-class starship, a half-dozen Armada-class destroyers, and enough Marines to subdue an entire system right on the doorstep of a Class-D planetoid inside Union space. Uninvited. A major breach of treaty. Not that the Empire has to care about the treaties they have with the backstabbers in the Union. But still. Not done every day.

Eight hours ago

The Empire sent a bunch of scientists down to the planetoid because the pampered brainiacs thought they'd found something to explain what's going on. Twenty Frontier Marines went with them. That was enough firepower to secure half the dinky little world.

Two hours ago

Communication was lost with the scientists and their escort team. All drones. All nets. Dead silent.

Now

It's tactical insertion time. Every Marine with a pulse and a pulse rifle is gearing up to go planet-side. That's where you come in, sweet cheeks. Wakey, wakey.

[END SITREP]

Lance Cpl. Lucky Lee Savage awoke from hypersleep, just as he had 156 times before.

He didn't know this yet. He didn't know anything yet.

He began his waking cycle the way he always did. Floating inside his mind, drowning, grasping for any thought, any detail—anything—that swirled toward him.

He was a Frontier Marine.

He was a planetary submission specialist.

He hated everyone.

He needed a weapon in his hand.

There he was.

Lucky opened his eyes and winced as blinding light spilled in around the hatch of the sleeping pod.

Facts of the mission appeared in his mind. Every useless detail compartmentalized for him, including the knowledge this was just the latest in a long string of high-G stasis sleep cycles.

This one would be no different than the last;

Wake up.

Do the mission.

Go back in the box.

"And good morning to you, too, Sunshine," said a female voice in his mind.

[2]
ROCKY

HIS HEAD POUNDED. His body ached. He smelled. And he was already tired of the info-dump flowing into his brain courtesy of his Augmented Neural Network, which he and every other Marine in basic tech training was told to call ANN, but they all just referred to as their AI copilot.

He called his Rocky.

"Excuse you. I call myself Rocky. You didn't name me. I'm not your pet."

"You're in my head. It's my call."

"I'm stuck in here. Not my choice."

"We're Marines. We don't get choices."

Lucky rubbed his neck, craning from side to side to appraise the other pods in the chamber, some already open. To his immediate left he spotted a kid fumbling with his sleepsuit.

Lucky knew a rookie when he saw one. It might have been a hundred years since he'd been one himself, but he still remembered that feeling. Glancing around at everyone else, feigned nonchalance while watching them disengage from their hypersleep pod because he had forgotten how. Being a rookie sucked.

Lucky nodded at the kid and purposefully pulled his accessory kit clear of his cooling system. The kid nodded back, waited a beat for Lucky to look away, then undid his own kit.

"Only twenty years in biological time, old man popsicle," Rocky said. *"Besides, you spent fifty percent of that on ice in an escape pod."*

"Don't remind me."

Rocky continued uploading mission data into his mind while prepping his organic systems for a planetary drop. He felt a stimulant cocktail hit his system, and simultaneously thanked and cursed whoever the military geniuses were that'd come up with the state-of-the-art artificial intelligence systems now grafted into his body.

In theory, Rocky and Lucky were two separate beings. Rocky lived in a neural pocket in his brain that didn't share direct pathways with his thoughts. In boot, they'd taught him to use mental constructs. The mind's eye was a virtual HUD where his AI could display anything from weapons status to drone's-eye views. The echo channel was where he could direct mental communications with his AI. All his trainers stressed that the AI could not literally read his mind or use his senses. They only had the drones and the biobots.

Bullshit.

The mental tricks were all just a load of mumbo-jumbo make-believe. So was the idea that there existed some red line between him and his AI. Maybe at boot, when the AI was just installed and simply followed all the rules. But Lucky knew better now.

Rocky could read his mind any time she wanted, and half the time knew what he was thinking before he did.

Reassurances from some Marine nano-technician in a clean white lab coat was *not* going to change his mind about that.

"Like reading your mind is hard," she echoed.

There was no 'mute' on the echo channel. Typical Marine design flaw.

He stripped off the sleepsuit and its cooling tubes to reveal his naked body. It felt strange not wearing combat armor.

The room was cool, but the stimulants kept him warm. His muscles burned.

"Must be colder in here than I thought," someone said.

Rocky sniggered.

Did other guys have AIs that enjoyed dick jokes? Lucky didn't think so.

He looked up to see a tight shock of blond hair atop a dark brown head. The naked man was facing away from him, but he didn't need to see the face to know it was Dawson.

Not that he remembered him. After every sleep cycle he woke freezer burned, his short-term memory a big bucket of nothing. He could never remember his last few missions. Rocky kept all his personal interactions filed away and updated his mind instantly when needed.

"If you wanted to remember shit," Rocky said, *"you'd remember shit."*

Lucky knew Dawson talked a big game, but also knew he was a light touch. He was shacking up with a fellow Marine Lucky had fooled around with years ago. Scuttlebutt was they had a daughter living with family on one of the Asiatic Ring worlds.

Frontier Marines weren't allowed to pair off, and they definitely weren't permitted to have kids. Not that Lucky disapproved. The less the brass knew, the better.

"You're not dead yet, Dawson?"

The head turned to reveal a big, stupid face. Always happy-go-lucky, this one. "Just lucky, I guess."

Lucky gave him the finger as he pulled out his combat dive gear. "Anyone else from the 153rd here?" he asked.

Dawson shot him a quizzical look. "I transferred. 58th now. Remember?"

"Oh right, my bad," he said.

Dawson seemed to connect the dots. "What the hell you doing here, anyway? Last I heard, the 153rd was on the Red front."

"Right, right," Lucky said.

He thought for a beat.

"Why the hell are *we here?"* he echoed to Rocky.

"That's above both our pay grades."

Lucky felt the familiar sensation as his internal nanobots went to work. His skin shimmered and shifted and slid aside as two-dozen dura-alloy plugs appeared on his arms, legs and chest.

He snapped his combat gear into the exposed plugs with practiced ease, and felt the skin flow back around the base of the connection as millions of tiny electrical shocks leapt from his skeleton across the armor and back again. The bots felt happy.

"Positive contact," confirmed Rocky.

Lucky felt for the punch pistol on his shoulder, then checked the handle of his pulse rifle on his thigh. Damn, that made him feel better.

"So much phallic love."

"Stow it, calculator."

[3]

EGGHEADS

On the ansible screen opposite his pod, a baby-faced lieutenant straight out of command school recounted all the facts of the mission that had just been uplinked into his brain.

Someone forgot to tell him this wasn't a recovery room for common grunts. Everyone here was an elite augmented Marine. With millions of credits worth of Empire tech crammed into their heads, each of the Frontier Marine could single-handedly command and control a thousand-drone army.

"Some of them even pilot starships," Rocky chimed in. This was a sore spot. She wanted so badly to fly ships. He barely had ambition to get up in the mornings.

Lucky took the bait, like the fool he was. Maybe if he kept it light ... *"Assist,"* he replied with a healthy dose of snark. *"You mean assist in piloting starships."*

"Oh, please."

Truth was, humans couldn't wrap their minds around the thought of AIs piloting the entire Empire fleet. Soldiers wouldn't get on those ships. Admirals wouldn't use them. No, that was unacceptable. There had to be some kind of human input.

So using Frontier Marines made everyone happy. The fleet got the benefit of using AIs—which screwed up way less than humans—but everyone could still sleep at night knowing humans were in charge.

The dirty little secret every Frontier Marine knew, of course, was that the AI really didn't need jack from the meat bag they were packed into.

The secret to piloting a starship for a Frontier Marine was just to get out of the way.

"There's more to life than starships."

He knew it was a mistake even as he echoed the thought.

Rocky leapt on it.

"There are 40,000 AI-enabled starships above Octavia-class in the Empire fleet," she rattled off. *"There are a quarter million Frontier Marines rotating among them. On any given day, those Frontier Marines engage in more controlled jumps, planetary insertions and open space combat scenarios than any million ground-and-pound soldiers. But no, you're right, there is more to life than piloting starships."*

"*Exactly*," Lucky said, now sheepish. His day wasn't getting better.

"Instead, we keep making combat insertions with the privates. Even though we have more experience than any dozen of them and you are twice their age—"

"But," Lucky started to object.

"—and I'm not counting biological age. And I have to watch their AIs graduate to destroyers while I end up on

backwater mining colonies, coordinating the shitty drones that keep your ass alive."

Not untrue.

"You know, those pilots rotate into ground assignments," he replied.

Also true. The act of piloting was mentally exhausting, but it wasn't conducive to a Marine's life. If you lived long enough as a Marine, you earned the right to get fat and lazy. But few of them did.

"With your insubordinate ass, that's all we get."

Ouch.

Lucky understood. He had a body. The perks of being a meat bag. She did not. A starship was something tangible, under her control. Unlike Lucky, who stubbornly refused to follow her every command, a ship was a direct extension of the AI.

Something flashed and the vid image changed.

A severe-looking woman in a white lab coat replaced the lieutenant. Lucky realized he was looking at a video from before the landing party had gone silent.

The woman's eyes lost focus for a moment as her eyelids fluttered. Then she spoke, and something about her seemed familiar. She was inside a plastic tent with light bots floating around. Just past the flapping tarp edge Lucky made out the base of a hastily constructed building and a couple of old Union-make rovers. Nothing Marine-issued, though. This was either recorded right after they'd landed, or the party was traveling very light.

Next to her stood a man waving a gloved hand over a very expensive-looking six-dimensional data cube. Lucky looked closer and saw it wasn't in fact a glove. It was a modified hand. A cyborg. Typical. Scientists get all the good toys.

His face was beet red, like he'd just finished a vigorous

workout before setting to work. But Lucky soon realized he was flushed with rage.

"That's about as angry as I've seen an egghead in a lab coat," he said aloud to nobody in particular.

"Somebody must've moved his beakers," said a Marine while doing push-ups.

The scientist was still speaking, gesturing at her angry colleague, and it was something Lucky knew he should care about. But screw the brainiacs.

Oh yeah, that chemical cocktail was doing the job. He liked how angry he felt.

"By the way, I'm not a Marine. I'm an augmented neural system composed of a trillion-trillion nanoprocessors throughout your body."

Rocky murmured on in his head as she had throughout his military life. All his life, really.

He took a second to pick up the thread of conversation she was referring to, then he dropped it.

"Just keep me up to speed, will ya?"

"Sure. You're in trouble."

"What's that supposed to mean?"

Before Rocky could answer, a loud voice cut through the recovery chamber.

"Man, hypersleep gives me gas."

Lucky heard grunts and groans as someone launched something across the room. The Marine scratched his balls as he sat on the edge of his chamber, the top half of his sleepsuit hanging off.

Lucky liked him immediately.

"Everything gives you gas, Malby."

Lucky turned to the new voice. Female. Stenciled on her combat gear bag, the name Jiang.

"How's it hanging, Lucky," she said without looking up.

Jiang was short and muscular and already sweating from a vigorous workout. She looked like she could handle herself. Something about her drew him in, but damned if could figure out what.

Lucky didn't have data on her, so assumed he hadn't worked a cycle with her.

"It's all still there," Lucky said.

In fact, he'd had a momentary thought that he'd lost an arm last cycle. Right below the elbow. He looked down. It was fine. Everything grows back on a Frontier Marine. Eventually.

That's the upside to having nanobots crawling all through your body.

"Lucky Savage? No shit?" said Malby.

He felt eyes move his way. Murmurs followed.

Malby strutted over like a peacock with his ass in the air.

"My buddy jumped with you," he said, looking around to see who else was watching.

Lucky changed his opinion instantly.

"So you're the Marine the brass can't kill," Malby said with mock admiration, sliding the towel back and forth around his neck.

Dawson had his combat gear on already. He walked past, ignoring Malby.

A Marine with Cheeky stitched on his sleepsuit took the bait. "The Butcher?"

"The Butcher," agreed Malby, grinning.

"But here's the thing," he said, lowering his voice conspiratorially. "My buddy said it's a bunch of bull. There ain't nothing special about you."

Lucky extended his arms, checking the seals on his combat gear.

Jiang finished her workout and started applying her own gear. "Malby, didn't you spend most of your last mission in regeneration stasis after you shot yourself?"

Someone laughed.

"I didn't shoot myself; somebody shot me," he snapped. "In the back."

Jiang smiled without looking up. "I'm sure it was an accident."

"All I'm saying," Malby continued, "is somebody named Savage ought to be a lot tougher than this joker."

"Guess I'm tough enough in a fight," Lucky said.

"You don't look tough to me."

"We aren't in a fight." Lucky stood up, checked the scope on his rifle, and holstered it. "Yet." He winked.

Malby puffed out his cheeks and looked like he might take a swing at Lucky. Then he laughed and rolled his eyes.

"Whatever," he said.

Lucky walked out of the recovery room and into staging.

"I liked him," Rocky said cheerily.

What had he called him? The Butcher? When had that one cropped up?

He was so sick of the stories.

The Marine the brass couldn't kill.

The warrior who survives every mission.

The ultimate lifer.

What a load of BS.

Everybody knew Lucky's story; lone survivor of a mission gone wrong, found alive after fifty years in hypersleep.

Now he was indestructible, the charmed one, forever lucky.

Nobody wanted to hear the real story.

In that version, he watched as his ship was destroyed and his friends were slaughtered.

Then he was captured. Experimented on. Tortured.

Finally, he escaped, half-dead and plagued by demons.

He didn't feel lucky.

[4]

HAMMERHEADS

"GOOD MORNING, MY POPSICLES!" screamed a voice Lucky recognized from another lifetime. Sergeant Peters. Alive, and ugly as ever. Even nanobots couldn't fix a face that hastily put together.

"Gear up and fall in, ladies. Today is a glorious day in the service of our Empire, as is every day!"

Peters surveyed the recovery room of groggy Marines with the stupid grin of a kid who just received his first pulse rifle.

"Once again you sorry bunch are the tip of the spear. We go first, the rest of the fleet follows."

"Oohrah," managed a couple Marines.

"We're the only Marines on mission point. So look alive!"

"Or look dead," chimed a few more Marines.

The only Marines on point. For an op this big. There was an entire armada out there.

Lucky glanced around, but only Jiang seemed puzzled. The rest were just going with it.

"We're it?" Lucky asked. "Just us and the fodder?"

A couple Marines smirked at the slang for Empire regulars. The sergeant didn't.

"Stop thinking, Lucky. It makes you look stupid."

Malby snorted loudly.

"Move it, assholes! I want priority drop in ten mikes! High-G, crash protocol, drones out, hammerhead approach!"

A thaw and leap assignment had its perks.

"At least I don't have to talk to anyone," he thought to Rocky.

"Present company excepted, of course," she replied.

He'd always pictured Rocky's trillions of nano-minions inside his mind as tiny spiders laying down impossible webs of targeting data, defensive positions, and operational information every trillionth of a second.

Lucky sensed the familiar old combat fear welling up in him. A little pit of anxiety that formed a perfect sphere he felt pressing against his abdomen.

He pushed it down.

Fight first, fear later, his sister always used to say. She had lots of sayings like that. Did older sisters just get a handbook or something? Maybe it was just a stick jockey thing.

She was a born pilot. Notched more combat kills in six months than he had in a dozen cycles.

She should be the one they told stories about.

But she was gone now.

After so many deep sleep cycles, his long-term memory was everything his short-term memory wasn't; totally baked in. He couldn't forget her if he wanted to.

And he desperately did.

Hypersleep stasis was a fact of life in the prolonged high-G FTL burns, but that's not why the Empire froze their Frontier Marines. They wanted to scrape their money's worth out of them. Non-mission time was time their precious super troopers were aging for no reason.

Freeze 'em and preserve 'em. Even a super trooper was just another cog in the massive machine.

Lucky watched as the rookie in the pod next to him puked. First freezes are tough.

The puke was nothing but green bile, but he managed to dribble it down his face and onto his gear.

Thank the universe he didn't have to jump with the rookies. He might be a lifer who didn't give two shits about promotion, but at least he'd been doing this long enough that he got to jump with the rest of the competent grunts who didn't get dead the second they touched dirt.

"First dive?" asked Cheeky.

The kid wiped his face with the back of his hand and nodded.

"Just trust your AI," said Jiang. "They do all the work anyway."

"And stick close to Lucky," Cheeky said.

"But not too close," Jiang countered. She wasn't smiling. She seemed to know Lucky a little too well.

"She has dived with me before," he shot to Rocky.

"Don't worry about it," she replied.

Well, well. It wasn't the first time she'd kept personnel info from him.

Cheeky stared at Jiang's backside with appreciation. She saw him out of the corner of her eye and mouthed something. Cheeky went red.

"Yeah, right," snorted Malby. "Just because that lucky bastard always makes it means nothing for the rest of us."

There was a general murmur of agreement about that.

"Nobody lives forever," Lucky said flatly. He stared

Malby down, but the asshole just blew him a kiss and went back to pulling on his gear.

"I really, really like him," said Rocky.

Lucky glanced back to the kid, who was struggling with his gear. Couldn't be more than sixteen.

"Jiang's right. Your AI will handle everything for you."

Jiang arched an eyebrow. "I was talking about the dive. It takes decades to fully mesh with your AI."

Lucky paused at that. His AI had been a mess when he first got it. But by the time he was revived from his deep freeze, it meshed perfectly. It had saved his life over and over again. His AI was what made him Lucky. He had spoken to other augmented Marines about this before. They always agreed that AIs were life savers, but Lucky got the impression they never meant it as literally as he did.

"I'm just that amazing."

"Sure you are."

They didn't seem to get as much flak from their AIs, either.

"Constructive criticism."

"Sure, it is."

In fact, other Marines didn't seem to argue with their AIs at all. Just gave them orders, and they complied.

Silence.

"Lucky!" screamed Peters in his ear. He flinched. "How long has it been? Ten years?"

"Sarge," he said.

Peters smiled easily. "Look how nice you clean up! No black eyes or broken teeth or drool anywhere on you!"

"Told you that you were in trouble," Rocky said, smug as ever.

"Now, I know you're going to pull some sob story about being freezer burned. Can't remember a thing. But my AI is in fine shape, Lucky," he said, smacking himself in the head. "Yes, sir, I'm watching a fine little screening of you liberally applying your fists to the face of a senior officer in the mess on Rikon on your last cycle. Ring any bells? No, of course not. Lucky, Lucky, Lucky."

He stepped closer and whispered. "We haven't worked together for a few cycles, so let me remind you. I run a tight fucking ship. How the hell you haven't been flushed by now, I don't know. You got special requested for this mission. Somebody at fleet keeps looking out for you."

Behind Peters, Malby mouthed "special requested" and pantomimed jacking off.

"But keep at it, and I'll shoot you in the back myself."

"Another satisfied member of the fan club," observed Rocky.

He ignored her.

His last cycle was Rikon? And this was Union space? He was on the wrong side of the galaxy.

He snapped the base of his hammerhead assembly in place with one swing of his arm, then jammed the locks with the butt of his pulse cannon without looking at him. Better to get to the drop hangar before he said what he thought.

"Yes, sir!" he said sharply.

The hammerhead was an orbital entry attachment that made it possible to jump from space to planet in a handful of minutes. It plugged straight onto his combat armor, adding limited ion thrusters and even more limited glide ability. The armor itself plugged into the exposed plugs up and down his body that ran straight through to his dura-alloy skeleton. It was an impressive piece of tech that made him look comically top heavy.

Point it down and dive. Even a Marine could figure it out.

"Clean contact," echoed Rocky. *"Positive control."*

He was about to shove on his helmet when Peters spoke again.

"You got a jump buddy, Lucky?"

Lucky froze. He searched desperately in his mind, plucking at the web of information Rocky had downloaded. Of course he had one assigned. He had to. Couldn't jump without one. He heard Rocky laughing in the corner of his mind.

"No, sir."

Peters smiled. The bastard knew it. Then he looked over his shoulder at the puking kid.

Oh hell, no.

"Private Nico, you're with Lucky."

He felt his teeth clench, and Rocky released a second cocktail into his system to cope with the spike in blood pressure.

"Yes, sir!" snapped the private immediately, then tripped, sprawling forward over his hammerhead, the same gear he'd just puked on.

Someone laughed.

Lucky looked down at the rookie.

"Gear up. I want to be diving in two minutes."

The kid's eyes went wide. He had the hammerhead over his head and shoulders but still hadn't managed to snap it into his combat plugs.

Next to the "this side up" message on the private's gear someone had scratched the words "this side fucked" with an arrow pointing the other way.

"This one's gonna get me killed," he said to Rocky.

[5]
NEW ROMA

He turned and headed for the hatch to the jump hangar.

The rookie followed, still struggling with his gear.

They were halfway there when Lucky saw Jiang, Dawson, Cheeky and Malby all standing around one of the big ansible screens.

"This is crazy."

"What did she do?"

"Desertion. Or Dereliction. One of the D's," said Malby with a shrug. "She's hot, though. Fifty credits says she doesn't last thirty seconds."

Without taking her eyes off the screen, Jiang flipped Malby the bird. He smirked.

Lucky shouldered Malby out of the way.

"Fuck off," he said.

"What are we watching?"

"Some seriously messed up shit," replied Dawson in his twangy drawl. For once, the smile was gone.

Lucky didn't get what the big deal was. The ansible feed showed a public execution in one of the lesser Coliseums on New Roma, no doubt devoted to one of the trendy new gods. Huge marble columns rose into the night sky. A very fine venue.

But the crowd was sparse. Did it really warrant a feed?

This poor soul was pitted against three-dozen mechanized combat bots. That was enough firepower to wage a small war. He wondered what could justify such a show of force. And then he saw why.

Behind him, he heard the rookie draw in a sharp breath.

"No way," Lucky heard himself mutter under his breath.

She was a Frontier Marine.

"Way, tough guy," said Malby, elbowing his way back in.

She had been stripped of her armor. But the legion number tattooed on her neck was plain to see. 5th Legion.

Damn, thought Lucky.

That was one of the Peacekeeper Legions stationed on New Roma. They were generally hated by the population. But then again, Frontier Marines were pretty much hated everywhere else in the galaxy, so why not at home? And somebody had to keep the population in line. More than twenty Legions were stationed on New Roma at any given time.

Lucky had never been to the Empire home world, but it looked nice. If you were rich. And well-connected. And lots of other things that Lucky was not.

The Marine had now been dodging around for a good dozen seconds. Malby might just lose that bet.

One of the drones got in a clean shot as she tried to maneuver around one of the defensive posts scattered about the killing ground.

Oh well.

She bounced around like a puppet under the heavy

barrage of slugs. Lucky winced. Her nanobots would repress her pain receptors, but she had to know she was done for now. She couldn't move with that much damage.

She staggered, and one of the battle drones finally found a good angle for its big pulse pluggers and fired.

At the last moment, she yanked her head backwards, and Lucky could almost feel the heat of the pulse on his own face as it sliced through air in front her hers.

But a second drone fired in the same instant. Perhaps in armor, maybe with some luck, she might have managed to dodge that too. But she had neither.

She was torn in half, her torso flipping into the air like a leaf on the wind. The drones didn't quit their assault, and the shower of slugs shredded her airborne upper body like a rag doll until there weren't even enough pieces left to see.

Her smoldering legs were all that remained.

The battle drone, apparently offended that any part of her was still recognizable as meat, fired another pulse. The rest of her disintegrated, along with a healthy chunk of the coliseum's dirt surface.

Malby let out a low whistle. "Niiiiiice." He slapped Lucky on the back. "Another pilot rotation just opened up."

This was new. Soldiers were sometimes killed in the executions. But Lucky had never heard of a Frontier Marine buying it this way. The Empire treated them like royalty. They spent untold trillions of credits on building and refining them.

"We're officially old news," said Cheeky.

"C'mon, she was just a screw up," chided Jiang, though she didn't sound like she was convincing herself, let along anyone else.

"Word is the Elites are almost ready," said Malby.

Ah, the Elites. For a bunch of entitled assholes who

thought they were hot shit, the Frontier Marines sure seemed worried about being replaced by the next big thing.

"That word has been around for as long as you've been a dick, Malby."

"No, its legit," said Cheeky.

"The blood eyes rolled out something last month. A first batch. Prototypes."

"Says who?" Lucky asked, doubtful.

Dawson shrugged. "People."

"Let me know when your people aren't full of it."

Just then, a red-eyed Empire scientist walked past. Like all clones, the red eyes were a mutation purposefully bred in.

The scientist didn't react to hearing the "blood eyes" slur, if he had it at all. Lucky didn't care. He hated scientists, cloned or otherwise.

"Well, how else to explain that little show?" Dawson asked. "They're sending a message. We aren't special anymore."

They were all silent.

"Move it, Marines," barked Peters, who'd appeared out of nowhere and blew past the group, heading for the hanger.

Jiang snapped on her jump helmet and followed.

The rest of the group turned toward the hangar, lost in their own thoughts.

Lucky had just reached the jump doors when he felt a tremor in the floor.

"Did you feel—"

And then the floor dropped out from under them.

"Fuuuu—" screamed Malby.

The lights flashed red and a high-pitched klaxon screamed in their ears.

A single word flashed in Lucky's mind's eye, transmitted no doubt through the internal AIs of every Marine around him.

B-R-E-A-C-H

The Marines scattered.

Lucky instinctively grabbed the rookie as the floor came violently back under his feet and slammed the kid down as he braced his armor against a crack in the wall panel next to the lift doors.

He grabbed his dive helmet, pulled it toward his head, and almost had it on when the ground dropped out from under him again.

The helmet cracked against his jaw and shoulder as he slammed into the ceiling that had inexplicably come crashing down upon him.

Stars flashed at the periphery of his vision and he wondered for a brief moment if they were real or just in his mind. He was on the edge of consciousness.

And then the lights went out.

[6]
GO

Rocky activated the infrareds in his eyes, and Lucky was treated to a view of gear and Marines floating among what was left of the staging room, which wasn't much.

The business end of a pulse rifle floated by his face, and he pushed it away.

Gravity was gone.

Oxygen was thinning fast.

He didn't yet have his helmet fully sealed, but Rocky had seen to it that his organic systems were protected with nano-mesh.

The walls had buckled inward, and the collapsed ceiling exposed a mess of wires and energy transfer lines. Gas poured in from the wall opposite Lucky.

"We've got radiation," said Rocky, all business now. *"I've activated shielding. Estimated time to lethal dosage is just under an hour, but it's going to be a real pain in the ass in ten minutes."*

The alarms had fallen silent with the lights, and they hadn't come back up. That was worrisome.

"Time to get off this bucket."

He snapped his helmet lock and heard voices on the all-comm from the scattered floating Marines.

"Damn, Tanner, you alright?"

"Still got gas, Malby?"

"Get this off me."

One voice boomed above the din. "Mission has not changed, ladies. We jump," bellowed Peters. "We jump now!"

Lucky took a second to digest this. Peters got higher priority data than anyone on the jump carrier. If they were still jumping, then some serious shit was going down.

"Oh yeah," echoed Rocky. *"It's fubar out there. I don't have full data, but there is clearly fleet-wide damage occurring. I've lost the broad net. Just weak local now."*

That was bad news. The Marines' AI copilots formed local networks to coordinate actions. Those nets should always be relatively strong as long as you were within a thousand klicks of other augmented Marines. And the last time Lucky had checked, this mission was stacked with them.

Internal AI never went offline unless a good chunk of your internal organs went offline, which was generally considered bad.

Lucky grabbed the rookie by his hair. *He didn't even get his helmet on,* he thought.

The kid's AI saved him, as it had many of the Marines, by instantaneously pumping nano-mesh over their skin to seal the vacuum and reduce radiation damage. All Nico's facial features were covered by a fine skin flap, rendering him blind, deaf, and dumb. He was only alive because of the mesh.

But the idiot still should've had his helmet on by now.

Peters knew exactly how useless the kid was when he threw Lucky into babysitting duty.

"Let's move!"

Nico shook his head and tried talking through the mesh. It might mean he was panicking. It might mean he was deep in discussion with his AI. Probably getting yelled at by his AI to get a helmet on, that it couldn't keep regenerating damaged cells forever.

Lucky punched him.

He couldn't see it, but he imagined red snot oozed from Nico's broken nose for a second before the nanobots staunched the flow and began knitting the bone and cartilage back in place. But it was going to take a few minutes for those teeth to regen.

"Gear up, dammit!" he screamed in his face.

He reached down and grabbed a hammerhead helmet—he had no idea if it was his—and slammed it over the kid's head. The seals slapped shut automatically, and as it pressurized, the skin flap covering his facial orifices slid back to reveal a stunned, wide-eyed kid with a crooked nose.

Lucky shoved him forward into the jump hangar. He wasn't above using fresh meat as a shield.

The hangar was just a gaping hole. No techs to do final checks. No chutes to dive through. In fact, not a hangar at all. Just a huge ragged hole in the side of what was now a dead box in space.

So long, jump carrier Beetle IV. He hadn't known the name of the carrier a moment before, but it showed up in his mind when he searched for it, in the way uploaded mission data tended to. He saw it was assigned to the destroyer *Argyle*. Never heard of that either. Fleet command mixed and matched these boats, just like the Marines they stuffed in them.

It didn't help he was on the wrong side of the galaxy jumping with a legion he didn't know.

"Go!" he screamed and pushed clear of the side of the transport, tumbling off in the direction of the yellow-brown Class-D planetoid they had come all this way to dance with.

"Not exactly the way they draw up jumps in combat school," observed Rocky, helpful as always.

Lucky wished he had time to appreciate what a total cluster this old jump carrier had turned into, but now wasn't the time.

He did anyway.

The spiders in his head simply could not resist patterns. Find them. Build them. Follow them. For better or worse, his head was full of pattern-recognition wetware that never turned off.

"Outward explosion pattern," reported Rocky. The spiders liked her better.

"So what?"

"So this was an internal detonation."

It was possible the damage had concealed an entry point from outside the ship. But his spiders didn't think so, and that was enough for Rocky. And him.

It was an internal detonation.

Miraculously, the kid seemed to get his bearings in the zero-G. Lucky suspected he had ceded all control to his AI copilot.

Lucky let inertia flip him around so he had a better view of the jump carrier, as Rocky slapped a magnified view in his mind's eye. He knew his relationship with the data was more of a direct neural flow, but that was freaking hard to wrap his tiny brain around. He wasn't paid enough to think that hard.

The damage wasn't isolated to the port side. The entire topside was crippled beyond repair.

He watched a set of Marines jump. Then another.

A single point of light burned Lucky's eyes. Radiation.

"*Drive is going critical,*" announced Rocky.

"*No kidding.*"

Four tiny figures appeared at the hole in the jump hangar.

And then they were gone, sucked inward as the carrier ripped apart.

[7]
NEW TARGET

The hammerhead thrusters pushed him and Nico toward the planet in an ever-steepening dive.

In the silence of space, Lucky watched the carrier erupt, its millions of carefully machined parts flooding outward into the heavens as deadly projectiles.

Lucky felt his arm shift slightly. Rocky was deploying his locusts. Tiny disk-shaped drones poured out from the back of his jumpsuit and mixed with a burgeoning cloud that spilled out of the rookie's suit and other nearby Marines.

The AI copilots of the diving Marines coordinated the drones and began picking off projectiles. His pattern-recognition spiders bounced around in his head at the pure joy of the chaotic feast of data, finding their happy place in the trillions of permutations.

Damn crazy technology.

There was a reason the Union dirt lovers were afraid of it. Then again, they were afraid of everything new. And easy. Always the crappiest life on the crappiest-class planets. Way to build a civilization.

Lucky flipped his all-comm open.

"Sound off. Who we got?"

"Jiang here."

"What the hell was that?" said Malby.

"Nice sound off."

"Shove it, Jiang. This is so screwed up."

"Nico, sir!" said the rookie, too enthusiastic for the party.

"Cheeky."

"Dawson."

They were sliding into classic two-by-two defensive waves coordinated by their AI systems.

"What the hell just happened, man?" Malby repeated.

"Something fucked up," said Jiang.

"Internal," Lucky said. "Maybe mechanical?"

"Wait, what?" Malby shot back.

"Didn't your AI see it? Those explosions. Definitely internal."

"Man, my AI ain't telling me shit," said Malby. "Net is down. I got no chatter."

Lucky waited for the others to chime in.

"Jiang, what about you?"

"What about what?"

"Did your AI pick up on the explosion pattern?"

"Negative," she said. "But I'm not surprised yours did."

"What's that supposed to mean?"

She didn't answer.

"What about you, Sarge? Any word from priority net before it went tits up?"

Priority net would be high command orders. The word from the top.

"Sarge?" said Lucky.

No response. Could it really be? Had the masochistic, misogynistic, pig-sticking son of a bitch actually bought it?

"Who in the almighty corps told you to count off, Lucky?"

No, he wasn't *that* lucky.

"Just here to help, Sarge."

"Help less, navigate more. New target. Tighten up. We go in hot, drones out."

New target? He must've gotten something from the brass, then.

"Have a look," said Rocky.

A magnified image appeared in his mind's eye. A simple rectangular building with blast marks along its perimeter that looked to be several stories tall stood at the edge of a ridge that dipped into a deep crater. Immediately inside the crater, nearest the building, a steep, rocky peak climbed out so that its top reached above the crater lip.

"I don't pick the targets," said Rocky, preempting any comments from him. *"I just point your sorry ass at 'em."*

Field tents on one flank told Lucky this was where the first landing party had touched dirt and set up a perimeter. He recognized several grounded stingray rail-gun drones holding position about a quarter klick around the building. But no Marines. No scientists.

"No local net," confirmed Rocky.

The original mission dossier called for a step-by-step approach. Lucky and the rookies here were to go in and establish the perimeter for the platform cannons already in transit. Or supposed to be. What exactly was in transit now was up in the air.

Probably a bunch of tiny pieces up in the air now.

He felt another set of stims hit his system as his nanobots began shifting his biological internals to account for the increasing Gs. The Marines would look like fireballs to an observer, even entering the thin atmosphere of the small planetoid.

"What's the sitrep here? What else is in transit?" Lucky asked on all-comm.

He could already hear the slur in his speech. This was biological, and there wasn't much he could do about it—not much his AI could do about it except monitor his organic systems.

He wouldn't black out. That was virtually impossible with everything in his system. But he would feel himself start slipping away.

Drift, they called it. Everyone who did combat jumps experienced it. There was just no reason not to push further than clear consciousness would allow when you possessed an internal AI copilot who could manage the jump just fine without operator input.

But it still sucked.

He got no answer from the comms, but Rocky's voice chimed in.

"Not much. I don't have ... of a network at this point, but I'm not sure if that's because... didn't get a coordinated jump, or..."

Damn, he was drifting now. Feeling the Gs.

He started seeing stars in his peripheral vision again, mingling this time with the ones already there.

His mind started to wander.

He knew where it would go.

The same place it always went.

His nightmare.

His hell.

[8]
DRIFT

HELLO, nightmare.

Hello, Lucky, said his nightmare.

But he wasn't Lucky. Just plain old Private Lee Savage, the adopted son of Admiral T'Hap, the little brother of the best pilot in the corps, a rookie on his first cycle, ready to prove he was all that.

Lucky woke up and just wanted to breathe.

He was drowning. There was green-yellow liquid over his face, filling his eyes, his nose, his mouth.

He tried to reach up, but his hands wouldn't move.

He tried to yell, but his mouth wouldn't open.

He was frozen inside a tank of gel, staring upward into a vast open space.

He could see something just at the edge of his sight, above and behind him.

He couldn't understand what he was looking at.

They were symbols more alien than anything he had ever seen carved into a rock wall. No, not carved.

Embedded somehow, like they were a growth in the rock itself.

He was sure the symbols were a language, but he couldn't explain why. As he watched, they morphed into letters he could understand. But the words made no sense.

The ceiling was higher than any hangar he had ever been in. The other walls were formed of rock too, but so far away he couldn't make out any details. Scaffolding criss-crossed everywhere he looked.

This was a massive space carved into rock. So big, clouds had formed inside it.

Not clouds. Smoke.

A flickering in the haze. A burning smell.

And then he saw the flames licking up the side of the tank he was in. Everything around him was burning.

He strained to move.

He screamed at his body, but nothing happened.

This is where I'm going to die, he thought.

Not in his fighter.

Not alongside his sister.

Here, in some impossible excavation site in a vat of snot.

He tried accessing his AI copilot—the one they told him during basic training would be with him for the rest of his life—but he only got static. He was alone in his mind.

Some Frontier Marine he was turning out to be. Captured on his first real mission.

He strained to remember something. Anything. The past was a haze.

An image flowed in from his subconscious. A creature stood over him, tool in hand, digging inside his mind. Shivers of electricity fired up and down his spine.

Had that really happened, or was it a dream?

He tried to steady himself by tying together stray moments in his mind.

He *had* been in his training fighter. He remembered that much.

They were attacked by ... something. What was it? He couldn't remember, maybe didn't want to remember.

It was just dumb luck that he'd been out with the alert fighters when their carrier was hit, the token rookie taking his turn with the big kids. Dumb luck that he wasn't dead.

But now Lee realized it had been very bad luck.

A shadow crossed his face. A red cloud darkened the edges of his vision.

He jumped, or tried to. Nothing happened.

Then he felt the tiniest of shocks on the back of his neck.

Next he felt the goo around him draining away.

And he could move.

So move, dammit!

He jerked up and felt wires yank back against his neck and head.

He reached behind, and to his horror found something like an umbilical cord with hundreds of wires wrapped in a fine mesh digging into pinpoints in the back of his neck.

And then he felt the ground shift, and a giant hand reached out and swatted him across the room. He felt his head recoil as the wires ripped away. The tank he'd been lying in flew across the room. The rocky ground beneath him was cold against his naked body.

Around him, equipment was burning. Strange, foreign gear. Not Empire tech.

Something exploded near him, and he felt heat flare from it. He tried staggering to his feet and immediately fell back. It felt like he hadn't walked in weeks.

The smoke was thick now. He tasted burnt air flow into his lungs. He put his face down to the cool floor and gagged.

He crawled blindly, tears filling his bloodshot eyes.

A shadow again crossed his face. This time, he reached out as the red cloud darkened the edges of his vision.

His hand bumped something.

It was the tank, flipped over in front of him.

If he could just get under it, there would be an air pocket. A second to think. Something.

He clawed at the edges, felt it fall back, clawed again and felt the edge lift. He thrust his face into the crack and took a clear breath, a cough wracking his chest.

He dragged his shoulders and the rest of his body under the lip. He finally yanked his feet inside, and the edge crashed back to the rock, creating an imperfect seal but keeping the majority of the killing smoke at bay.

He took another clear breath.

Now what?

Now you leave dreamland, Lucky. See you soon.

Lucky shivered. He knew the voice. It was Him.

It was The Hate.

[9]
SCREWED

LUCKY AWOKE to Rocky's voice.

"More trouble."

"What—"

A bright light burned a hole in his vision. Pain radiated from his eyes, invading his mind.

His head snapped back into the padding of his helmet.

His faceplate darkened as new stimulants entered his system, and his eyes itched for an intense second. He realized his retina had just been scorched and repaired.

"Holy bastard, will you look at that," said Malby.

Lucky was looking, all right, but he didn't believe what he was seeing.

It wasn't every day you saw an Occupier-class starship explode.

"Altchinger drives," he said.

They were the largest power source in the region, probably in all of Union space.

But it should have been impossible. With so much shielding and so many safeties in place it was damn near impossible for the drives to go nova.

But the universe likes a good challenge.

In the vacuum of deep space, the destruction was a haunting sight.

At ten klicks from bow to stern, there had been a literal city inside. The starship was the *Lindleson*. The city was—or had been—New Promise.

The city name meant more to him than the starship.

"Rocky, did I—"

Lucky blinked, and a handful of memories appeared.

He remembered drinking in a shitty bar there on a mission three cycles back and getting into a fight with a pack of stuck-up Navy blackshoes and then buying a couple of them drinks later on. He remembered screwing one of them and thinking it would've been more fun if she didn't have a brace on her busted arm.

He remembered sitting in plenty of bars there, watching tanks patrol the streets and druggies begging for credits.

And now, it was gone. New Promise had always lived at the mercy of her starship. It was a city of soldiers who knew the risks.

But you'd still rather have your hand on the stick when it was your turn to go. Nobody wanted to die in their sleep. No soldiers, anyway.

Those poor assholes didn't know jack.

"Holy hell," said Malby.

"Gods in Olympus," said Jiang. "There were a million souls onboard."

"Anybody know the drivers?" asked Cheeky over all-comm.

On a ship of that size, typically two or three Frontier Marines would coordinate flight responsibilities. There was an entire ecosystem of near-ship activity buzzing about endlessly.

"Patterson and Milky for sure. Not sure who else was on rotation..." Jiang trailed off. "Well, I guess it doesn't matter. They're all dead now."

"Everybody was on the Lindleson," said Dawson. "Command. Everybody."

Lucky picked up on the sadness in Dawson's voice. He wasn't talking about the sector Admiralty.

He heard more heavy breathing from someone. Maybe the rookie. Maybe all of them.

"KIT, Marines," said Peters. "Keep it together."

Malby respectfully declined to do so. "We're screwed, man!" he screamed in all-comm. "Totally screwed. What the hell's going on? This can't happen. This can't be happening, man!"

"Enough, Private!" barked Peters. "We have a job to do, and we're inbound to do it. So look alive."

"Or look dead," several Marines said in unison.

He wasn't wrong. There was nothing they could do now.

Plus, Lucky didn't give a shit about that old can or anybody on it.

Hell, man, what is wrong with you, Lucky thought.

"What isn't wrong with you?" said Rocky.

He knew combat stimulants were partly to blame. The cocktails he was pumped full of after the escape from the Beetle IV left him full of rage. Not fear. Not concern. Not even focus as far as Lucky could tell.

Just rage.

He also wondered how much of that was actually the stims in his system and how much of that was really just him.

So, there was something wrong with him. That wasn't new.

But there was something wrong with this whole operation. The Empire didn't screw up like this.

And putting a force this huge inside Union space for a tactical insertion? That wasn't just strange. It was wrong.

Sure, the Union couldn't do anything about it. Even when their whole system wasn't going off the grid, they barely had the tech to spit in the Empire's eye.

But it was still a giant middle finger. And look what it got them.

"We're gonna need a new way home," Rocky said.

The Empire had less than a hundred FTL starships. It was more than any other power in the known universe, but still.

To lose one in Union space seemed impossible—like a baby knocking out a professional fighter.

Also, the *Lindleson* was the only source of the bubble field essential for the rest of the armada to navigate the distortions in space back home. Without it, the entire fleet was stuck at sub-light speed.

Not that there was much armada left.

Lucky watched the fireworks through the lens of the spiders dancing in his head, an endless web of lines and permutations as chunks of debris bounced and exploded and ricocheted in new directions through space, tearing silent, deadly wakes in everything they passed through.

He soon registered the patterns as coming from more than one source, even as they spread chaotically. His spiders concurred.

"Odd," he echoed.

The destroyers nearer the *Lindleson* had been caught in her wash, but several farther out had suffered secondary explosions of their own.

In fact, there remained only a handful of intact destroyers in near-space. That didn't make any sense.

"Same pattern as the Beetle IV," said Rocky.

Internal detonations. Sabotage. Has to be.

"Rocky—"

"Already on it," she interrupted.

"Better send that through priority net."

"Priority net is down too."

That was the worst news of all.

The priority net was the high-orbit network of drones that facilitated armada-wide chatter. Even with this fubar fun going on, they should be unaffected.

It could simply be interference from the blast.

Or someone could be knocking out high-orbit drones.

Lucky knew what his money would be on.

"On that note," Rocky said, *"we seriously need to consider cover support."*

Lucky pulled up the data Rocky had pieced together and cursed under his breath.

"Sarge, we got nothing sending signatures from the surface."

He waited for a response. Data from his combat suit told him the pressure was changing outside. They were picking up some ionizing chop in the thin atmosphere. Their options were diminishing fast.

A dark rage rumbled inside him, clawing to get out. He fought it down.

"Sarge?"

"I heard you Lucky. Stand by."

Now Malby jumped in. "Wait, there's nothing down there? Nothing?"

Lucky was already evaluating the situation in his head. This was bad. Not terrible. Not yet, anyway. Even without heavy support weapons, seven Frontier Marines were a formidable force.

Thanks to AI implants and drone tech, a single field operator could run an effective force equivalent to multiple non-AI divisions.

Lucky shuddered at the thought of deploying with a full division of non-augmented Marines. He could only stand so many of his fellow Marines as it was.

A guy needs elbow room.

"Always warm and fuzzy thoughts with you, eh?" said Rocky.

"Get the hell out of my thoughts."

"Occupational hazard. I'm giving you a fresh cocktail."

"More drugs. My hero."

"Two minutes to glide status."

"Let me know when—"

"Contacts!" cried Malby.

[10]
SKREAMERS

Lucky pulled his head out of his ass and scanned the surface.

The Marines were at angels one five and falling fast.

The hammerhead was no longer providing thrust, just glide support thanks to a set of small airfoils that had materialized as their speed slowed.

His locust drones had come home to ride out the entry and weren't yet redeployed. That wouldn't be a problem under normal circumstances, since they'd be getting telemetry data from the high-orbit drones.

He hadn't bothered to use what meager net was still up. Neither, it seemed, had Rocky.

"What are you seeing, Malby?" he asked.

"In orbit, in orbit!" screamed Malby.

What the hell?

"Rocky, give me a look."

He couldn't turn his head back at this point, but Rocky ran the visuals from the skimpy network of local drones through his mind's eye.

The thin atmosphere offered an unbroken view into

space. Aided by the enhancers on the drones, the view was fuzzy but clear enough.

Union fighters were pouring into near orbit.

Skreamers. Highly maneuverable, single-occupant fighters.

Wherever skreamers were, though, bigger ships were sure to follow.

But he didn't see anything bigger up there yet.

"Where are they coming from? I don't have carrier contacts."

"They just showed up," Malby declared, and for the first time Lucky realized he was a tech specialist. Malby would be tapped into whatever was left of the rapidly disintegrating drone network that fed data to the whole armada.

"No larger contacts."

"Not possible," said Jiang flatly.

"What's that formation?" asked Cheeky.

Lucky saw it too and guessed Cheeky had fighter experience, same as him.

He watched as the skreamers lined up for strafing runs against the few destroyers left out there. But skreamers were no match for a destroyer, even a damaged one. It would take hundreds of runs just to make a scratch.

But the skreamers formed in a strange pattern, flying in tandem, wing to wing and in columns of five.

And then he watched as a blue energy surge appeared to jump forward from a point well in front of each skreamer, then merge and arc out lazily toward a destroyer. The energy then seemed to disappear through the massive starship and keep going.

A moment later, the destroyer began splitting into two clean halves as silent explosions raged across its bulk. Then all fell still.

Holy hell. What had he just seen?

"Rocky?"

"Assessing now. Definitely nothing we've seen out here before."

That much was certain. *The Union barely had the tech to wipe their asses. Where the hell did they get the firepower to gun down destroyers with a handful of fighters?*

He watched as a second formation came together and another beam of blue energy sliced through another destroyer.

Two more destroyers turned to intercept. A single beam cut through the stern of one and tore deeply into the hull of the second.

"Angels five," announced Jiang. Five klicks.

Lucky felt the puff of more locusts releasing from the back of his combat suit. It was time to assess the situation on the ground.

"I have something else now," said Malby, still patched into the orbital drone network.

Lucky wondered how the hell the private had this kind of access.

"Definitely bigger. But it just showed up like the fighters. I have no previous vector."

"FTL drop?"

"Negative, no signature for that. It just showed up."

"Any ID?" asked Dawson.

Lucky realized he hadn't heard from the rookie in a while, wondered if he was passed out. Or dead. Either way, his AI would take them to the planned coordinates. Nothing like touching down with a sack of dead meat, a not altogether uncommon occurrence in Lucky's experience.

"It's ... It's doing something," said Malby.

Lucky waited.

"A little more detail might be helpful, Malby."

"It's ... They have something that's ... that's burning up everything."

"Say again?"

"I've lost the network. I've lost all the fleet drones. I think everything in near orbit is gone."

Malby sounded shaken, his voice at a high pitch, and Lucky could almost hear the cocktails pouring into his system to bring his heart rate down.

"There was a pulse unlike anything I've never seen. Energy dispersion was off the charts. I need to crunch the numbers on it. My AI is saying that it just dissolved everything."

"Rocky, you getting his AI data?"

"Yes. Seemed like a controlled nuclear burst, but the yield was magnitudes beyond anything we've ever experienced before. And if I didn't know better, I'd say the pulse splintered the chain reaction, dispersing it to specific targets."

"But you do know better, so what was it?"

"That's my best guess."

"Seriously? Your best guess is that the Union, who swore off autonomous technology two-hundred years ago and hasn't had a weapon that could penetrate Empire armor in twice as long, just used a weapon out here that our scientists can only have wet dreams about?"

"That's what I'm saying. Except the wet dream part."

They were in full glide formation now. He felt the soft shifting of locust drones as the last ones dispersed from his dive suit. He already had a good view of the terrain below in his mind's eye.

"Sarge, this is a major problem. Not only do we have no

planet-side signatures; now we have hostiles above with no resistance. We're sitting ducks down here."

"We do have planet-side signatures, though," said Jiang.

"No—" Lucky started to say, then stopped.

But there were signatures down there. The drones could pick up weaker signals this close to the surface. Well, one tight cluster of them. They hadn't resolved fully yet.

They were right at the coordinates Peters had them diving for.

"Friendlies?"

From within his mind, he felt one of the spiders pluck a string of data. Without thinking, he dipped and his body slipped sideways, like a puppet answering the pull of a string. Something bright arced by his shoulder.

Not friendlies, then.

"Incoming!" he screamed. From the corner of his eye he saw the other Marines fan out in search of more maneuverability.

"Five seconds to close visual range," declared Rocky. *"If we can see them, they can see us."*

"Sarge," he said over direct-comm. "Suggest we alter coordinates two klicks south, come up low on their position."

Lucky didn't wait for a reply. He wasn't much for waiting on orders anyway.

"Nico, get on my six and look alive."

Lucky banked out of his dive.

"Rocky, find us somewhere to land, preferably away from—"

"Multiple incoming," Rocky stated, entirely too casually.

[11]
DEAD MEAT

His spiders began jumping around excitedly as lines of data streamed into his head.

Beams of blue energy leaped up around him and the other diving Marines, and he again felt the soft pull of his mind as he glided between two incoming vectors.

He gritted his teeth, knowing that with all the drugs he probably looked like a maniac.

Why the hell weren't these guys on scopes until they were right on top of us?

"Good question," agreed Rocky.

"Better question: What now?"

They couldn't do this all day, and certainly not as they got closer to the ground.

As it was they were easy pickings, with zero intel on the enemy signatures below and falling fast without any support from the ground or in the air. Even by Frontier Marine standards, this was a hot jump.

The terrain map in one part of his mind's eye wasn't much help either, the landscape generally flat with few natural barriers.

But man-made barriers were everywhere. He realized what he was looking at were hundreds upon hundreds of ground rovers, parked haphazardly everywhere.

It was as if everyone from every mining platform around had hopped in a rover and made straight for this part of the planet.

"Looks like someone decided to have a party and didn't invite us," said Malby.

"Typical," said Jiang.

"Sarge," Lucky said over direct-comm. "We gotta get out of this."

No response. Lucky sighed. It wasn't the first time a sergeant had left it to his lance corporal to run things. His superiors just couldn't seem to get it through their ladder-climbing skulls that Lucky didn't want to be in charge of anything more than his own neck.

Lucky spotted a relatively clear space amongst all the randomly parked rovers about a half click from where the concentrated fire originated.

"That's where we go, Marines. Hit it hard. Now," he barked over all-comm as Rocky painted the target into the mind's eye of the other AIs.

They all dived.

Except Peters.

"Sarge?"

He waited a beat.

"Are you screwing with me? I know it isn't the target, but c'mon! We don't stand a chance from the air."

Still nothing.

"He's dead meat falling," said Rocky.

She must have accessed his AI via the local net.

"How bad?"

"RTC in five minutes." Regeneration to consciousness.

"Bullshit. This will be over in two. Rocky, get his AI to override and land him with the rest of us."

"No can do. His internal injuries can't handle the Gs. AI is aiming for soft landing on the far side."

Lucky glided up next to Peters.

Both his legs were broken and twisted, bouncing off the back of his hammerhead wing. Whatever they were shooting at them from the surface, it has sliced through his alloy armor like it wasn't there.

It's just not possible, he thought. The Union had nothing that could do this.

Inside Peters' body, he knew trillions of biobots were furiously working to restore his vital organs to health. He hated the old asshole, but he was a good boss on the ground. At least he had been the last time he'd put boots on the ground with him.

More than anything, Lucky did not want to be the most senior guy left down here. That scared the hell out of him.

"This is suicide. He'll be cut to pieces on a slow approach. Can we circle?"

"For five minutes? No, we're in full glide now. In fact, we can only stay up another minute."

The other Marines were diving for the clearing in the haphazard maze of rovers. He watched the flare of their hammerheads reversing thrust as their AIs waited until the last possible second to fire hot bursts that brought them to a stop inches from the ground.

He imagined the stimulants hitting his own bloodstream as the cocktail fought to keep the Marines conscious and aware as the sudden hard-G landing rattled every joint in their bodies.

Everybody else was having all the fun.

"Here comes some fun," said Rocky.

With the other Marines on the ground, Lucky, Nico and Peters were the only targets airborne.

A dozen blue energy beams filled his forward view.

[12]
PANCAKE

Lucky let his spiders do the work, reacting to their signals.

He juked hard to port, watched a beam scream over his shoulder, then rolled over two more of the blue energy beams.

He checked his six and was pleasantly surprised to see the kid holding his own.

Rocky pinpointed and enhanced an image from one of his drones positioned near the base of the structure down there.

Lucky recognized the building as a stackshack, one of the Union's fast deployment bases. It was an ugly square block of a structure, with interlocking levels flanked by external ladderwells on either side.

These stackshacks, however, were tougher than they looked, with reinforced dura-alloy walls and heavily secured airlocks. They weren't fortresses, but shacks were decent defensive positions in a pinch.

Abandoned equipment lined the exterior ladderwell closest to Lucky. It looked like the landing team had set up operations at the base of the building then bullied their way up to a higher floor.

Some sort of weapon sat atop the ladderwell now. He didn't recognize it, but it was clearly Union build. Far more advanced Union build than he had ever read intel on, and he again thought of the Union skreamers taking out their destroyers in orbit.

Five firing canons sat on two tracks with a single operator in the middle.

Lucky took a good long look at the man sitting between the twin cannons. Middle-aged, fat, and balding, and wearing miner's overalls.

What he wasn't wearing was any body armor.

What the hell?

"Rocky, have your locust fire on him."

The locusts had relatively weak ordnance onboard, but were more than capable of cutting through flesh.

The image wavered as the locust fired a pulse.

Two more of Rocky's locusts nearby fired off pulses of their own.

They all bounced harmlessly away.

The operator was clearly protected by an active energy shield that probably secured the whole platform. It meant a direct attack with anything other than a battle cannon was probably useless.

What he wouldn't give to have all his ordnance flying down with him. Too bad it was in little pieces in orbit.

He took another look at the ladderwell. It was little more than scaffolding.

"I've got a bad idea," he murmured.

"Lucky," chirped Rocky in a warning tone.

"Yes, Mother?"

That shut her up.

"Nico, stick with Sarge," he said.

He didn't look back to see if he was dead meat, too. If he was, so be it. This was no longer babysitting territory.

"Yes, sir," came the crisp reply.

He pushed his nose farther over.

He was seconds from running out of glide space.

The building came screaming into view.

He didn't have any weapons. Except himself and his thrusters.

Five seconds.

Red mist crept at the edge of his vision and he willed it away. Anger bubbled up, biding its time. Lucky couldn't keep it at bay forever in these conditions.

"Rocky, keep the demon in the bottle," he said.

He aimed for the base of the scaffolding.

It dawned on him these were the exact coordinates he was supposed to be landing at.

How happy his superiors would be to see him following orders to the letter.

Four seconds.

"Wait until the last moment to fire those reverse thrusters."

"You're going to be sliced in half by one of those supports."

"Good talk."

Three seconds.

The crosshatch side of the scaffolding loomed up. It suddenly didn't seem so funny.

Just as he began to line up on one of the supports, out the corner of his eye he saw the cannon belch an energy beam.

It was a blur just fractions from him.

Two seconds.

Too close!

He knew he wouldn't be able to dodge from this distance. He gave himself over to the spiders, allowing them to yank him like a marionette. He felt his body swing violently as a burning tore through his thigh.

One second.

He opened his eyes and felt a wave of nausea as his body was thrown viciously forward, flames coursing around the edges of his vision from the shoulder exhaust vents of the hammerhead.

A metallic shriek rang in his ears, jerking his head to the side as a sickening thud brought him to a sudden stop, pain searing through his left shoulder.

Something above him was driving his head downward, bending him impossibly forward. A snap, and he felt his body swing fiercely back. Something hollow and metallic arced past his head, and he caught a momentary glance of scaffolding collapsing downward, pancaking one section at a time.

Closer. Closer. Closer.

His prone body started bouncing as the platform around him shuttered. He felt the spiders tugging at his mind, willing him to move.

"Again, Rocky. Hit them again!" he yelled aloud, hoping she'd understand.

A moment later, his hammerhead landing rockets fired again, spending the last precious drops of energy in the landing capsules.

He felt his weight shift, but it wasn't enough. His legs were still pinned.

He stared up and saw the second-level platform give way.

He pushed with all his might on the flat scaffolding

pinning him down, felt it shift one last time as the last level collapsed.

He rolled over as the last of the onrushing pancaking sections reached the ground with a tremendous roar of air and pressure.

Dirt and rock kicked up wildly around him as the force of the collapse ejected him outward and over a lip next to what remained of the foundation the scaffolding was built upon.

An explosion erupted as the Union energy weapon finally succumbed to the same planetary gravity that had toppled the rest. Part of the cannon flipped over, spewing out the middle-aged man who'd been operating it. His face was melted raw, and his eyes were gone.

Lucky almost missed the weapon until it was too late, but his spiders caught the danger and he leapt off his feet, swinging his own pulse rifle up as he did so. A blue energy beam belched from the man's gun, but his aim was poor.

Lucky's aim was not. The man's head snapped back and he toppled over.

Lucky knelt and scanned around the base of the stack-shack as Rocky ran through his bio damage. A fresh chemical cocktail hit his bloodstream as he sensed the bots quietly knitting his thigh back in place like hidden hands stitching a loose quilt back into shape. The sensation tickled.

Two boots appeared next to him.

He swung around, pulling his rifle to his shoulder for a snapshot.

The boots were Marine boots.

He relaxed and looked up into the serene face of Sergeant Peters, head hanging forward, seemingly asleep.

His AI had carefully glided him into position directly onto the landing coordinates at the base of the building.

His hammerhead jets maneuvered to shift the Sergeant into a sitting position.

Lucky saw his leg joints were already repaired, bending slightly as he sat.

He slumped over.

Lucky bastard, he thought.

Peters opened his eyes, unfocused and bewildered for a moment.

Then he locked on Lucky and squinted.

"I should've known," he said.

Lucky shook his head and lowered his pulse rifle.

"You're welcome."

And then Peters' head exploded.

[13]

BLIND

Lucky instinctively ducked and felt heat searing just beyond his head. He smelled singed hair and for a split second thought it was his own until he realized it emanated from the wafting crater of steam that had been the location of Peters' brain. His skull, right down to the blood-spurting stump of a neck, was now pulverized.

There were many, many places you could shoot a Frontier Marine and it would grow back.

This was not one of them.

The stream of blue energy stopped, and Lucky threw Peters' body to his right as he rolled to his left, calling on his drones to once again give him a fix on the location of the energy blast.

It was not what he expected.

He saw a long-haired child in miner's overalls emerging from the back cab of a nearby rover. A girl, no more than eight or nine-years-old, he guessed.

She held a long curved blaster that encased her arm almost to the elbow. It had a thick rounded middle that tapered out to a larger opening at the end, about the size of her fist. It was smooth and reflective and didn't appear to have any obvious sighting mechanism.

She held it at arm's length like an extension of her body and fired without any noticeable effort to aim it.

If this was a Union blaster, it had none of the ineffectiveness that label would imply.

The blue energy it emitted poured out in a constant stream so that the beam whipped around as the muzzle shifted, slicing into anything it came into contact with.

Perhaps owing to the success of the blue energy he'd seen earlier, he shouldn't have been surprised by its effectiveness. But Lucky was still stunned.

Of all the armor a Frontier Marine employed, his skull was still the most important. His AI copilot was biotech in his head. It was the central command center for both his drone army and his biological support functions. A blow to the brain killed the Marine, killed any chance of recovery, and killed all operational effectiveness in theater.

By contrast, even a mortal blow elsewhere on the body that could not be healed by nanobots would still leave the AI copilot alive and functioning for several hours, depending on how long it took for all electro-biological function to stop in the human.

That was why AI copilots were instructed to deliver their operators to their targets, even if their wounds were too severe for regeneration. Battles had been won by Frontier Marines long after they died.

For those reasons, the helmet was the most carefully crafted article of defensive gear, designed to disperse all known forms of energy, channeling it outward along its edge and away from the vital brain pan.

This blaster had simply sliced through Peters' head and

kept slicing onward, almost taking out Lucky in the process. Dumb luck had saved him for the millionth time.

Again, he was looking at an enemy with an incredibly effective weapon with no apparent defensive interest. She wore no armor and made no attempt to protect herself.

The girl shuffled forward in a blood-soaked dress and filthy socks.

Lucky felt a stirring in his stomach that told him the girl's blaster would fire again.

He squeezed off two rounds from his pulse rifle and dove wildly, willing his drones to triangulate on the central point in his target and bend the pulse in midair to find it.

The girl was cut down where she stood, the pulse shredding her small body.

She'd still managed to send the firing impulse to her finger, but her nearly severed arm fired wildly upward, glancing harmlessly off the side of the stackshack several floors up.

She didn't move, but Lucky wasn't convinced she was dead. He held his rifle at his shoulder and gripped tight. He took a halting breath. Then another.

Then he stepped slowly toward the girl.

He had hit her center mass, nowhere near her face, and yet there was caked blood there.

Her eyes had been gouged out of her head. Violently.

"What the hell's going on, Rocky?"

"Her aim was remarkably good, all things considered," said Rocky.

"Is that supposed to be funny?"

"No, quite the opposite. Clearly she was blind before she shot at you."

Before he could answer, a shadow flitted across his vision.

He again spun, rifle raised to his shoulder.

Nico executed a textbook high-G approach, retro boosters firing him to a midair stop before dropping him hard on wobbly legs from nearly a meter up. To the kid's credit, he nailed the landing.

He was starting to grow on Lucky.

Then he slipped in the pool of Peters' blood at his feet and fell forward over the sergeant's slumped body.

And then something even more unexpected happened.

He heard a voice from heaven.

[14]
HIDDEN

"Hello! Marines?"

It wasn't over all-comm. It was wafting in and out of the thin atmosphere.

Lucky looked up at the sky, dumbfounded.

"I'm right here," the voice said, exasperated. "On the roof."

Lucky slowly turned his head to follow the sound.

Standing on a ledge of the stackshack where the top of the ladderwell had been was a man in a white lab coat.

It was the scientist from the vid earlier, the cyborg who'd been playing with the six-dimensional data cube. He looked as beet red and angry as the last time Lucky had seen him.

"We don't have all day. Can you please come in here?"

Lucky blinked.

"Is this really happening?" he thought at Rocky.

"It is," she confirmed.

It figured that the goddamned brainiacs would somehow pull through when everyone else was dead.

Lucky glanced back at Nico, who had crawled to his feet and was staring at Peters' body.

Lucky was about to distract the rookie so he didn't puke when he got an alert from his drones. Two more figures were climbing out of nearby rovers.

He ducked down, yanking the kid off his feet as he did so.

"AIM clearing maneuver," he said. "Step over and cross-check."

It was a classic tandem between two Marines with AI support that Nico should be well versed in. He nodded, probably glad to have something to do that he remembered from combat training.

Lucky crawled forward to the rover a woman had stepped out of and sent a drone in ahead of him. It reported no movement, then swung out to a covering position for Nico to slide open the rear cab door as Lucky stepped in with another trailing drone.

Nico followed and slid open the door on the side nearer the new targets, keeping his drone at his six and a firing space clear ahead of him.

A woman who had appeared dead in the passenger seat suddenly leapt forward with another smooth Union blaster. Lucky cut her down. He felt a heat signature to his right, then his spiders danced in his head and he jerked to his left and rolled back out of the cab as an energy arc sliced through the air where his head had been.

An old man was at the opposite end of the rover, leaning in through a hatch. A drone punched a hole in his arm, and the weapon toppled over, taking most of his arm with it.

Lucky glanced over at Nico, who had his rifle up with a clear shot. Inexplicably, the kid was watching Lucky roll back out of the rover instead of tearing the old man a fresh hole.

"Enjoying the show?" Lucky screamed.

Nico finally pulled the trigger on his pulse cannon, and the drones triangulated the shot into the center of the man's forehead.

The old man silently crumpled.

The kid stared forward, eyes unfocused and his eyelids fluttering. Lucky couldn't decide if he was in shock or just interacting with his AI. Either way, he didn't have time for this shit and took back his earlier assessment. The kid was an incompetent idiot.

The silence was broken by the scientist's his high-pitched voice wafting down from above again.

"Hey, did you hear me?"

The asshole wouldn't quit whining. *"Can you tell him to shut up?"*

"I have no networks to send a message to," Rocky replied. *"He either doesn't have neural networks or isn't using them. Either way, I can't help you. Unless you want me to have a drone shoot him."*

"Tempting."

He and Nico held their position, backs to the rover. Lucky wondered what surprises waited in the other rovers.

"This is why we couldn't see them," said Rocky.

Lucky was lost. The scientists? *"Who?"*

"Our targets. We got heat signatures late because they were sitting in those rovers, effectively shielded from our high-level scans."

She was right.

Every single rover littering the open field was a perfect hiding place for these things.

And with that came a realization.

He pictured the clearing he'd painted for the rest of the Marine dive team. It was right in the middle of a vast graveyard of these haphazardly parked rovers.

This is why I should never be left in charge, Lucky thought.

"Jiang, sitrep!" he screamed over all-comm.

No reply.

"Malby? Dawson?"

Nothing but cold static answered his call.

"Hang tight, we're inbound!" he shouted, hoping someone was receiving.

"Oh really?" said Rocky.

"Really. We aren't leaving them out there."

Rocky sighed.

"Drones out and hot."

Lucky heard a crackle and then something like pulse cannon fire roar over the all-comm. He heard a grunt that could pass for a response. It was all Lucky needed.

Lucky smacked Nico on the top of his helmet and pointed to the rover on his left. Lucky quickly slid behind the giant tire of the rover on his right. He pulled his rifle up and nodded at Nico.

"Do we have a plan?" asked Rocky.

"Sure we do," he answered, and at Nico, he yelled; "Light up anything that moves!"

[15]
SUICIDE

LUCKY ROLLED from behind the giant tire and ran forward at a low crouch for the next randomly parked rover a half-klick ahead of them. He felt a quick jolt from a stimulant cocktail. Five locust drones appeared in tight formation around Lucky as he tore forward.

Nico fell in behind him.

Lucky saw the drones begin to fire. It seemed like they all fired at once. And then came the reply, as streams of blue energy arced up from the rovers, cutting down drones in wide swaths across the sky. The drones were just as defenseless as the Unioners, and both sides quickly dwindled in number.

Just as quickly, the plan—if you could call it that—went to hell.

The kid took two steps, and a beam of blue light streamed out from below the rover Lucky had just been leaning against. His left foot severed, Nico screamed and fell awkwardly into the cab of the next rover along.

Lucky leapt into the air to avoid the same fate and fired

blindly as he jumped into the cab of a nearby rover, ready to fire on anything inside. But it was empty.

He slid across to the other side and glanced at the kid. He took a deep breath, jumped out of the cab, took two giant steps, then dove into the back of the rover Nico had fallen into. The kid's eyes were fluttering again, though this time Lucky was sure he was receiving a serious stimulant kick while his biobots went to work on his severed foot.

Lucky ripped a recovery bag from the kit he wore on his combat belt. In one practiced motion, he yanked the kid's bloody stump of a leg up and dropped it back in the bag and pulled tight the cinch. The organic material inside immediately activated, and the bag turned a radioactive green.

He would be mobile in twenty minutes and fully regen'd in a half hour.

The rest of the Marines out there would be dead, of course.

"This is suicide, Lucky," echoed Rocky. *"Even with a partner at your six. We've lost over half our drone cover. I can confirm 130 disabled targets, but it's not enough."*

In his mind's eye, he could see the terrain was still crawling with heat signatures. Arcs of light slashed through the sky as the drones returned fire with surgical strikes that were deadly to the defenseless miners. But for each that fell away, two more appeared.

"Dammit, there's no way we're leaving them out there," he screamed aloud.

He leapt out of the rover and ran a dozen feet over to the next empty cab.

A beam of blue energy lit up the ground where he'd just been, whipping along behind him as he ran.

"They're already dead," said a booming female voice from behind him.

He looked back to the base of the stackshack some twenty meters away.

A blast door that had been recessed into the wall and partially hidden by the scaffolding debris was suddenly open. Peering just over the lip was the scientist from the video.

She didn't look nearly as cool and calm now, but her voice was steady.

"If they aren't dead yet, they soon will be," she said.

"Sure are a lot of scientists around," observed Rocky.

"No shit. Were they all just in there singing songs together while the Marines were out here getting their asses kicked?"

Light illuminated the blast doors, but so far none of the eyeless fighters were shooting at it. That would change soon.

Perhaps sensing that, she ducked low and turned back into the blast doors.

"Hurry, we have to close this."

Lucky looked back the half-klick toward his Marines. "Screw you, lady," he murmured under his breath. *"Rocky, paint me a path."*

Lucky turned to Nico's rover a dozen feet away.

There was just a pool of blood.

He turned around. The kid was hopping on his one good foot toward the open blast doors.

"Nico, get your ass back over here!"

The kid stopped and looked back at Lucky, bewildered, his bio-sacked stump dangling pathetically in the air.

"Sir?"

Lucky gritted his teeth. "Get over here."

"Yes, sir!" screamed the kid as he swiveled and started

hopping back. His foot was several minutes away from any meaningful regeneration.

"It's not like Sir Hop-a-Long is going to help us," said Rocky.

"You stay out of this."

The scientist appeared at the blast door again, yelling something.

But Lucky wasn't interested in what anyone had to say anymore.

He heard more pulse fire over the all-comm. There was a firefight out there, and he had to get to it fast.

In his mind's eye, Rocky had illuminated a path through the maze of dead rovers.

The drones around him buzzed forward to cut down what they could.

The kid was still hopping his way back.

Rocky was right. He was more than useless.

"You'd better have one hell of a detailed sitrep waiting for me when I get back," Lucky said calmly over his shoulder.

"Sir?"

Lucky rolled out from behind the rover, pulling his pulse rifle to his shoulder and setting off at a full sprint between rovers.

The movement brought out two eyeless Unioners, but Rocky had expected that and had drones waiting for them.

A lazy stream of blue energy flowed wildly into the sky as one of them squeezed the trigger as it was cut down.

Lucky kept his head down. A spider plucked in his mind, jerking him left, then another pluck, and he juked right. He was a puppet on a string again, at the mercy of his pattern-recognition bots to keep him alive.

Two more arcs of blue light tore into a rover on his right, sending one of its huge tractor wheels spinning away.

Lucky pulled the trigger on his pulse rifle again and again, firing wildly and letting the drones find him targets. But more and more shots didn't curve away in any direction, and Lucky knew it was because there too few drones left to help triangulate his shots. He was on his own.

"It's time, Lucky."

"No, dammit, we can do this on our own."

Distracted, Lucky took a moment too long to react to the pluck of his spiders, and a searing burn ripped through his hip. He felt an instant of pain before his biobots overrode the nerve message to his brain.

Lucky stumbled and fell.

But he was not going to die here in this godforsaken hellhole of a backwater on the edge of Union space.

He crawled on all fours under a rover.

Warm signatures closed in. Another arc seared just above his head, smashing into the rover he was under, throwing it up on two wheels for a moment before crashing back down over him. The shocks gave, and Lucky felt a crunch from his armor as it absorbed as much of the blow as it could. He felt a crack in his chest.

Something's leaking under here, he thought.

"That's you," said Rocky, grimly.

Blood gushed from his hip while his biobots tried desperately to staunch the flow.

The cab door opened. A middle-aged man with gaping, blood-caked eye sockets and a bald head stepped out.

Lucky pulled up his rifle, then closed his fist on nothing but air. His rifle had slipped out of his feeble grasp.

He flopped forward like a dying fish, grabbed the man by the ankle, and yanked.

An arc hit the bottom lip of the rover just above his head as the man instinctively fired his weapon before his back hit the ground.

But this only made it worse, Lucky realized. Now the freak was at his level. The sprawling man swung his weapon around and pointed it in Lucky's face.

Lucky stared into the gaping muzzle and felt the warm crackle of energy wash over him.

[16]
PUPPETS

He missed.

Dirt exploded where the pulse left a hole next to his head.

The bastard missed him from point-blank range.

Something buzzed overhead like a blur.

A pulse hit the man as he squeezed the trigger a second time. The pulse caused him to flop up in the air, and his weapon discharged wildly into the side of the rover. It bounced up and back down again, and Lucky was again driven downward by the pressure of the rover. The blaster dropped from the man's grip and came to rest across the palm of his outstretched hand.

As Lucky stared, the man's finger reflexively closed one last time, brushing past the trigger as the gun finally slipped out of his grasp.

Lucky watched as another drone buzzed over. Then another.

"Nice work, Rocky."

"Not my drones."

"Then—"

Suddenly, the sky was full of locusts.

Lucky dragged himself upright, wheezing as his chest ached.

A sharp static burst hit the all-comm.

"Get down!"

It was Jiang's voice.

Lucky dove back to the ground, his ribs on fire, waiting for something to happen.

Then he realized she wasn't talking to him.

At the base of the stackshack, Nico rolled on his side as a Marine in hammerhead gear shot by in a blur.

Jiang bounced once as she skated across the dirt, twisting so that her hammerhead took the brunt of the blow. However, the move left her spinning out of control on the rebound.

She slammed shoulder-first into the side of the stack-shack with a sickening thud.

Dawson bounced off the edge of the rover Lucky was leaning against, coming to rest on his side, legs splayed back across the rover's huge back wheel assembly.

Matted blond hair and a big goofy smile filled the face-plate. "Incoming," he said, and swung his legs down as an arc of energy fired into the air, followed by another a second later.

Cheeky limped around the side of the rover opposite where Nico was now hiding.

"Ay dios mío!" screamed Cheeky, red cheeks quivering. "What the hell are those things?"

"They don't have eyes," said Nico helpfully.

"What the hell are those blasters? Never seen anything that powerful."

Lucky was still trying to come to grips with their sudden arrival.

"How—"

"Fuuuuuuuuuuuuuu—" came Malby's screaming voice across all-comm.

A moment later he landed, far less gracefully than Jiang had, and stupidly tried to put his hands and feet out to absorb the landing.

Lucky heard his leg snap.

Malby tumbled to a stop next to the stackshack, where Jiang had just gotten to her feet.

"Malby, you ass."

He grunted as his pain cocktail kicked in, then struggled up on his one good leg. Lucky counted several fingers pointing in a variety of directions, too, but as he watched biobots snapped them back into place.

Lucky scrambled up, holding his chest, and ran for the rover closest to the base of the building, coughing up blood as he went. He fired his rifle in wild arcs behind him, trusting that the renewed swarm of locust drones would keep the eyeless things busy for the moment.

"Hey, great idea about landing, genius!" Malby yelled. "Where the hell were you?"

Lucky looked over at Peters' headless body.

"Busy."

"Aw, damn," said Malby.

Jiang frowned and quickly shed the rest of her destroyed hammerhead.

Lucky realized they had pulled the same trick he had, using the last of their landing burn juice.

It got them airborne, if only a few dozen feet, so they could glide here.

But they had no way to stop.

Considering Jiang had been the first to arrive, and that

she was the only one with half a brain, he figured it was her idea.

"And this?" Jiang asked, motioning to the pile of rubble that had been the scaffolding and Union gun mount.

"Just another successful landing," he shrugged. "No crazier than your idea."

She raised an eyebrow. "Don't thank me." She nodded at Cheeky.

"Cheeky?" he said. "You crazy bastard."

It was his turn to shrug. "Me and my buddies used to take turns jumping off cliffs. We'd see how far we could go before we fired the jets to get back up. So I got a pretty good idea of how much juice they have." He smiled. "It's more than you think."

Lucky stared at him. "That's crazy."

"Nah," said Cheeky. "I mostly made it back out."

Lucky hadn't realized quite how much of a daredevil Cheeky was. He was impressed.

He turned back to Jiang and saw she was standing next to the inset blast doors.

They were closed again.

Lucky banged hard against them. "Hey! You in there? Open up."

The other Marines exchanged looks.

"One of the scientists is in there," he said. "Two of them, actually. They offered to let us in earlier." Lucky banged again.

Malby leapt to the doors in two bounds. "Hey! Hey! Hey!" he yelled, pounding with urgency.

Jiang joined in.

There was no response from the other side.

"Looks like they rolled the red carpet back up," said Rocky.

"Malby, think you can get us in there?"

The tech took one look at the airlock pad and shook his head. "It would take me more equipment than I have with me," he said. "These are battle hardened. They aren't made to be popped from the outside."

"Incoming!" yelled Dawson, no mirth in his voice this time.

Rocky and the other Marine AIs had pooled their drones, and the cloud of them had fanned out, looking to draw fire.

"Show me, Rocky."

The view in his mind's eye rapidly expanded as Rocky overlaid a grid of what their drones were seeing. Hundreds of warm targets began to converge on their coordinates.

"Not good. It looks like they are starting a coordinated move."

"What are those eyeless freaks?" asked Malby as he and Jiang joined Lucky and Dawson with their backs to the rover.

"Just puppets with guns," said a voice behind them.

They all looked back toward the blast doors, now tantalizingly open. A woman in a lab coat was silhouetted against the soft light emerging from within.

"Not that different to you."

[17]
XENOTECHNOLOGIC

As soon as the blast doors closed, Malby screamed and threw down his combat helmet. It bounced across an inner chamber that led into a small operations room. "What is happening?!" he yelled, waving his pulse rifle and hopping around as his broken leg healed. He looked at Jiang, then Lucky. "Where did the Union get blasters like that?"

Nico closed his eyes and slid down a mesh wall next to a bank of computers, waiting for his foot to finish regenerating.

Lucky looked closer at the computers and recognized them from the vid. One was the six-dimensional data cube that Mr. Beet Red had been using.

That seemed odd. In the vid, they were under the tarp outside the stackshack.

Lucky holstered his plasma rifle and slid down next to Nico.

Nico opened his eyes and glanced over at Lucky, then sat up straighter.

Lucky smiled. "You're all good, man."

Nico hesitated, then relaxed his shoulders.

"Sorry about being a dick out there," Lucky said.

Nico's eyes widened. "Nothing to apologize for, sir. I should never have gone for the blast doors."

Lucky silently agreed, but tried to put the kid at ease. "And you can stop with that sir crap. I'm no officer. I'm just old."

Nico nodded. He still had his hammerhead top on. It was warped and dented, but Lucky could still make out the "this side fucked" scratched on the side.

In the middle of the small operations room, perma-peacock Malby was still holding court.

They sat and watched for a while before Nico broke the silence.

"So, is it true?"

"Is what true?"

"You know," he said, "What they say about you?"

Nico squirmed, clearly not wanting to repeat what it was they were saying about him. "That... that you can dodge anything. That you never get shot."

"Maybe you missed the big hole I had in my thigh earlier?"

"Oh yeah," he said.

"Kid, I learned a long time ago that nothing good comes from paying attention to what people say about you," he said.

"He doesn't remember anything about anyone anyway," said Jiang, who had walked up while they were talking. She was sneaky.

The kid looked at her quizzically. "Why?"

"His short-term memory is toast after every cycle," she said.

"What the hell, Rocky?" he said. *"You gave me no data on her. It's pretty clear we've worked together before."*

And she knows me too well, he thought. This wasn't common knowledge.

Nico looked surprised. "Really?"

"I'm not exactly state-of-the-art, kid," he said.

"Oh. Because of the... because you were in stasis so long?"

"Fifty years in cryo will do that," he echoed to Rocky.

"Fifty years stuck in your head. I got the raw deal."

"Yeah, something like that."

"Don't you get tuned?" asked Nico.

"They can tune up the tech, but they can't do much with the meat," he said, smacking himself on the head.

"Ain't that the truth," Jiang mumbled.

But it wasn't the truth.

The truth was that he remembered more and more every day.

He was the opposite of an old man and his fading memories. His grew more vivid with time. The short-term burn of each cycle gave way to the long-term memories he couldn't forget.

When he was younger, he wanted the memories. He craved them.

He bragged and boasted. He didn't get his reputation by accident.

He'd list the actions he'd been in. The enemies he'd killed.

But somewhere along the way, the wars grew meaningless. The victories hollow. The ground bloodier.

Now he wanted to forget.

He wanted to forget the wars he'd fought in the blackness of space, in the bowels of space stations, on the ashes of dying planets.

He had fought all his life.

He'd seen men killed for nothing more than a look. Killed men himself for the same.

He'd killed men, women and children. Burned them alive, drowned them, tore them limb from limb and laughed over their carcasses.

He'd been a coward, a liar, a thief, a cheat. He'd cried and begged for mercy. He'd cursed those who asked for it in return.

He'd killed enemies in their sleep, as they ran away, as they took a piss. He'd killed friends who got in his way.

The universe would be better if he wasn't in it.

But he was.

"Look, I don't need to know what I did or what someone says I did," he said. "I just need to live to the next cycle."

Jiang shook her head. "It's no way to live," she said, then hesitated a moment. "And I know what you are capable of. Both good and ... bad."

"Rocky, you gotta give me something. How does she know me so well?"

"Like you are that hard to figure out."

"Seriously? What is she, like, blackmailing you?" he said.

Rocky was silent.

Great. Just great.

"My brother met Lucky here when he was a rookie, too," she said to Nico. "He pretty much worships the ground Lucky walks on."

Nico smiled at that.

"Or used to. He's dead now."

Nico's smile evaporated.

She absently rubbed the chain around her neck again. A

long, curved fang hung from it, the fossilized tooth a reddish brown. Jiang saw Lucky watching and stopped rubbing it and slid it back inside her combat plate.

It belonged to her brother. That much was obvious. But there was something else about it.

"He's got a soft spot; he just doesn't want anyone to know about it," she said. The words seemed forgiving, but her voice was sharp as a plasma edge.

"Don't believe everything you hear," Lucky said to Nico. "And don't try to be a hero. You'll be fine."

Jiang shot daggers at Lucky with her eyes. She stood up and swung a cheap elbow at him as she walked past.

Malby was still shouting, spittle flying from his mouth. "And what the hell was that in orbit? They cut our destroyers to pieces!"

"You tell us, Malby," said Jiang. "You're the tech specialist."

"You saw what my AI saw," shot back Malby. "No way the Union can do that. No way!"

Malby paced faster now, his leg having healed to a slight limp.

Cheeky and Dawson stood near the blast doors, eyeing the two scientists. The wound on Cheeky's thigh was almost gone.

Jiang was looking at Lucky like he should do something.

Like what? he thought. *Sarge is dead. Our support is gone. You want me running this shit show?*

"Well?" Malby said expectantly to everyone and no one.

"Is he just going to stand there shouting?" said the tall lead scientist curtly as she surveyed the Marines.

She was older. In her late fifties, Lucky guessed, although biological age and Empire standard age could differ wildly depending on how much time you spent in cryo.

Lucky knew all about that.

She had dark brown hair with gray streaks and looked fit as a drill sergeant and twice as stern.

"Looks like we have a new alpha in the group," said Rocky.

"Who are you, lady?" Malby exploded, taking two big steps toward the scientist.

She didn't flinch.

Dawson took two lanky steps of his own and smoothly stepped in front of Malby.

"Easy, baby," he said. "We're all rattled."

Malby stared for a second longer at the scientist, then gave Dawson a shove and turned around.

"So, who *is* in charge here?" asked the scientist.

Jiang looked at Lucky again.

"Guy outside without a head," said Lucky.

The scientist didn't skip a beat. "Well, who's next in command?" She tilted her head toward Lucky.

He closed his eyes. "You wouldn't be talking to me if you didn't know it was me, lady," he said.

Her colleague snorted. He had yet to look up from the data cube he was engaged with. His artificial hand was glowing, and his eyes were glazed over.

"Big and stupid," he said in a voice meant to carry. "What a surprise, Vlad."

Lucky recognized the voice as the idiot who had shouted down from the upper window.

"Thanks for all your help out there," said Lucky.

The scientist didn't look up, but he did shrug.

"I didn't realize you couldn't come and go like the other Marines," he said. "I don't know how your stupid toys work."

"Orton, please," said the old scientist.

"Vlad?" asked Jiang.

"Ah, yes, introductions are in order. My name is Vladlena Alyona. I'm the lead XT investigator on our expedition. But my team members just call me Vlad." She looked around, unsure for the first time. "My team is gone, of course. As are your comrades."

She paused again to clear her throat. "This is Davidson Orton, our lead data harvester."

Orton shook his angry red face but again refused to look up from his cube. He looked like a teenager, but Lucky knew he was older. Just a baby face. The kind of little punk who never grew up and needed a good ass-kicking.

Lucky's sister would have probably described Lucky that way, too, once upon a time.

"Charmed," said Lucky. "Where are your blood eyes?"

Vlad frowned at the insult. "Our clones didn't make it."

"So just the bloods bought it, eh?" he said, noting her again flinch at the word. "What a coincidence."

Scientists always got sensitive when you implied that they treated their clones badly. Even though they did.

Lucky named off the other Marines then turned back to Vlad.

"XT? Xenotechnologic? Since when does the Empire send relic hunters on secret missions?"

Orton finally looked up from his cube, shock on his face.

"Are you for real?" he asked. "Vlad is one of the smartest people in the universe. She has more brains in her little pinky than you have in your entire body."

"Hey, he doesn't even know me," said Rocky.

"Orton, please," said Vlad.

Orton kept staring at Lucky in what was supposed to be a menacing glare.

Lucky stifled a smile. He was always looking for a good fight, but hitting this kid would be like hitting a puppy.

Malby looked ready to explode.

"Now that we're all friends, what the hell is going on?"

Lucky nodded. "How about it, Vlad?"

She sighed. "I'm afraid I've gotten us all killed."

[18]
ANOMALY

Orton had just settled back to his data cube, but now he jumped up out of his seat, waving his glowing data-harvesting hand.

"No way," he said. "You cannot put this on yourself, Vlad. There's no way we could have known any of this was going on here."

"What *is* going on here?" Jiang asked.

The question hung in the air.

"We have known for some time that the Union was in possession of alien technology."

Lucky found himself leaning forward.

"What, like a relic?" asked Malby, incredulously. "All of this is from a relic?"

Vlad regarded him icily. "Obviously not. Relics are cold, dead artifacts of bygone civilizations. We find them all the time. What you see out there,"—she waved to the blast doors—"isn't coming from some trinkets on the black market."

It was true that humanity had been finding relics of past alien civilizations for as long as they had been exploring the stars. But those had all died out billions of years ago, more or less at the same time. A fact that really baffled all the smart people.

It didn't mean jack to Lucky.

What they hadn't found, despite all the expectations that they would, were any actual, living aliens.

This also meant nothing to Lucky. Few things did.

"Hold on," Lucky said, raising his hand. "So you think they found real, living, breathing aliens?"

"No ..." she hesitated. "Well, we didn't think so. Now we aren't so sure."

She looked at Orton, who had gone back to his data cube. He nodded absently. "I don't see anything here that appears to be xenorganic. We are strictly dealing with xenotechnologic evidence."

"Alien tech, but no actual aliens," stated Jiang, who was again absently rubbing the chain around her neck.

"Exactly," said Vlad.

"So, you're telling me that the Union found some working alien technology and that is what did this?" Malby said, incredulity in his voice.

"In so many words, yes."

"Bullshit."

"Can you shut up and let the lady talk?" said Cheeky.

"Make me," retorted Malby, turning on Cheeky.

"C'mon now," said Dawson, always the peacemaker.

Orton shook his head.

Lucky thought for a moment it was at the behavior of the Marines, but the squat little scientist was staring at his data cube.

"It just doesn't make sense," he said to Vlad. "There is no way this signal is related to the original anomaly. It must be the second one."

Vlad stepped behind Orton, and her eyelids fluttered as she accessed the data as well. Her rapid eye movements were distinctive. He remembered them from the vid.

"I don't think we got the full picture, yet," said Jiang.

Orton let out an exasperated sigh. "For the love of—"

"Orton!" warned Vlad.

"I'll just tell them, or they'll just keep acting like they're entitled to know, even if they can't understand," he said, staring down Malby who looked like he might knock the guy's teeth out.

Lucky couldn't help but notice none of the other Marines were standing between Orton and Malby this time.

"The Union has had alien tech for some time. We have known that. But we couldn't get any details because all our spies went dark. Complete communication silence. We used to know everything the Union was doing before their own commanders did, but now we were in the dark. We couldn't recruit new spies, and we couldn't send in our own. They just went dark immediately as well."

"This was all in our briefing. Isn't that the reason we're here?" asked Lucky.

Orton shook his head. "That's barely the half of it."

"Good to know the silencing of entire worlds is just the half of it," Dawson said.

Orton shrugged as if to agree, but Vlad stepped in before he could make things worse.

"We don't know what happened, but we don't think it's what it looks like," said Vlad.

"Well, it looks like they're all dead," said Jiang. "And I thought that was as bad as it could get for them until I saw this little creep show up out there."

"We think they are fine. There has been a military coup, of sorts," Vlad said.

She again hesitated, looking at Orton. For someone who had seemed so sure of herself a few minutes ago, now she was stuttering along.

"A military coup?" Jiang repeated.

Vlad nodded slowly, aware of the delicacy of explaining this fact to a well-armed member of her own military.

Orton showed no such tact.

"Regardless of the apes in charge," Orton said, waving dismissively, "What we are really concerned about is that whatever experiment they were running has gone wrong."

"Not necessarily wrong," interjected Vlad. "Perhaps it just expanded faster than intended."

Orton nodded deferentially. "Yes, that could be it," he said. "We didn't have any clues, and then we saw the sudden flare of activity around the anomaly here. We have known about it for some time, but there was nothing that made it special—"

"What anomaly?" Jiang cut him off.

"Don't you Marines talk to each other?" He waved his arms. "Didn't the first group of you explain what we found?"

Lucky wasn't interested in explaining the concept of need-to-know to this prick. And frankly, Lucky wouldn't have cared if he had known. "Explain it," he said.

Orton shrugged. "We found a spaceship."

[19]
SIGNALS

LUCKY WAITED FOR MORE. Orton wasn't offering.

"And—" he prodded.

Orton shrugged again. "There is nothing special about it. Typical relic."

He waved his hand at the data cube, and for the first time the three-dimensional view shifted from a number set into an image.

At first glance, it just looked like a piece of rock protruding from the dirt. A second longer, and Lucky realized he had already seen it. They all had. It was the steep rocky hill jutting out of the crater just beyond the stackshack.

Up close, everything changed. It wasn't a hill. It wasn't a natural formation at all. From ground level, the shape of a rock-hewn spacecraft was unmistakable. And enormous. And—

There was something vaguely familiar about it. Alarm bells started going off in his head, and suddenly he felt a wave of nausea wash over him. The edges of his vision were suddenly tinged with red.

Orton was droning on about how it was the kind of find a lesser research team could spend a lifetime poring over, but his team knew better. There was nothing special about it.

"Uh oh," said Rocky.

"Did you just hit me with a cocktail?" Lucky replied.

"We need to talk."

"Kinda in the middle of something here, Rocky."

"This can't wait."

"Well?"

"I'm having trouble controlling Him."

This was not what Lucky expected. He sat up straight.

Rocky didn't talk about The Hate often. She was as scared of Him as Lucky was, but she was the only thing standing between Him and complete control of Lucky.

"What do you mean?"

"I mean ever since we got here, He has gotten stronger. He wants out. I can feel it, and I don't know how long I can keep Him in."

"How has it gotten strong?"

"I'm not saying I have all the answers, Lucky. I don't even understand how He is here."

"Well I don't even know what He is."

"The point is, if it gets out down here, I don't know if I can put it back in the bottle."

The Hate had saved his life more times than he could count. But it was pure evil. When it took over, Lucky couldn't control himself. He wanted to kill and maim. He was uncontrollable. He didn't differentiate between friend and foe. He wanted everything to die.

Something inside of him was a cold-blooded murderer. A demon.

Each time Lucky asked for its help, he vowed it was the last.

But he couldn't stop making deals with the devil.

"The nightmares are getting worse, too," he said.

Were they? *Yes*, he thought. He hadn't realized it until he said it, but it was true.

"The drift dream about the experiments? I thought you always had those."

"There was something different about this one. It was more ... real. Vivid. I don't know how to explain it. I was there."

Rocky seemed to be turning this over.

Like The Hate, the experiments weren't something either of them liked to talk about.

Before the experiments, he had been just a rookie with a typical AI.

After the experiments, he and Rocky became ... intertwined. He was able to coordinate with Rocky in ways he didn't hear other Marines discuss.

They were probably both in denial.

"Think for yourself, buddy," she said. *"And besides, we know they're connected."*

"We are all connected," he said.

Rocky didn't disagree.

The Hate. The experiments. It was a puzzle he had never been able to put together.

He also couldn't make any of it go away. No matter how many times he burned his memories, they always came back.

He knew they always would.

Lucky was startled out of his dark thoughts by the sound of laughter.

"Hell, Malby," Jiang said, shaking her head.

“Why is that funny? It’s a spaceship. It might still work.”

Orton took a turn at rolling his eyes.

“It’s eight billion years old and encrusted in rock and ore. What do you think?” he asked. He didn’t wait for a response. “Obviously not. It’s a relic.”

Malby pointed at the blast doors with his pulse rifle. He still hadn’t put it down.

“Then what do the Union weirdos want with it?”

Orton squirmed uncomfortably.

“That’s what we were trying to figure out,” said Vlad.

“They aren’t related,” barked Orton. He looked at Vlad hesitantly. “They aren’t related,” he repeated more softly.

Vlad said nothing.

Malby blew his top. “They aren’t related?” he screamed. “They sure as hell look related to me! Or did you not see all the rovers on the damn planet congregating here for a giant party?”

“That is what I’m trying to tell you. The signal that’s controlling them is coming from the other anomaly.”

Lucky jumped back into the conversation. “Hold it. There’s a signal? And another anomaly?”

“Yes,” said Vlad. “We tracked it as soon as we landed here. We didn’t realize what it was doing at first. They didn’t attack until the main team had gone to the original anomaly site. There is some Trojan horse at work in the rudimentary Union wetware.”

The Union might have hated tech, but they still wanted to control their population like any good power did. So they had basic nanobots implanted in all their citizens. They provided simple functionality—basic biobots for disease and injury, docility and loyalty impulses, the usual. But their stuff still sucked.

"So, they are getting hijacked and going nuts and pulling their eyes out?" asked Malby.

"Yes, but it isn't nuts," said Vlad. "Vision takes up an inordinate amount of mental functioning. The Trojan needs that to receive and interpret the signals. It compensates with other senses. Like I said, these aren't people anymore. They are programmed puppets."

"And the other anomaly?"

"That is more speculative," Vlad said, looking over at Orton. "Whatever it is, we have triangulated the position of where the signals are originating. It is a point in space."

"What's there?"

She shrugged. "We don't know. We don't exactly have resources in orbit at the moment."

She waited a beat. "But we'd sure like to find out."

No one spoke for a moment.

Jiang was still fixated on the eyeless freaks outside. "So, this is what all the citizens of the Union look like? This is why we lost contact with their home system?" She was shaking her head.

But Vlad cut her off. "We know for a fact that isn't the case. We've lost our spies, but those we have smuggled in have been able to provide us with some information. We have reports of these puppets in the population, but this is strictly a military operation."

Lucky assumed the spies were actually unmarked clones. That was against every treaty in the universe, but trivial issues like that wouldn't put off the Empire.

"No military would go along with doing this to their civilian population," said Cheeky.

"Said the planetary submission specialist," replied Orton.

Cheeky glared, but Lucky just leaned back and caught Jiang's eye.

She raised an eyebrow.

"The mil-tech was the first to be trojaned," explained Vlad. "And it was easier since they have networked AI capabilities. Once they were in the military network, gaining control of the military leadership was ... simple." She shrugged in apology. "And soldiers do what they are told to do."

Lucky flipped her a middle finger but didn't get into it. "Okay, so some are following orders. And some are mindless puppets like them," Lucky said, nodding at the blast door. "Who is pulling all the strings?"

"That is precisely what we came down here in the first place to try and figure out," she said.

Lucky flipped the sighting bar on his unholstered punch pistol up and down while he thought about it.

He looked over at Jiang. He could tell she was thinking the same thing.

"Nah," said Lucky, hand coming to rest on the small firearm. "I don't buy it."

[20]
TIME'S UP

"What is that supposed to mean?" said Orton, looking around incredulously.

Vlad didn't say anything, but her eye darted to the punch pistol in his lap.

"I think you're trying really hard to make me think you care about who is behind this. But I don't think you care at all, or maybe you do, but the Empire sure as hell doesn't."

"Please enlighten us," said Orton, sarcastically throwing his arms up in the air.

Lucky holstered the punch pistol. Orton really was oblivious to the implied threat, like a puppy that had never been kicked. It was almost endearing.

Orton crossed his arms and tilted his head.

Jiang beat Lucky to the punch. "Take it from someone who has been playing for this team for a while. We didn't come out here because the Empire gives two shits about the Union's civilian populations."

Lucky was annoyed, but nodded.

"Exactly," he said. "The Empire cares about two things. New weapons and old wars. I think the Empire knew the

Union was trying to weaponize some alien tech. But they figured the Union couldn't find their ass without help—a fair assumption—and didn't take it seriously. But now, it's looking like the tech-averse dirt lovers might have actually made a breakthrough. And that has the Empire brass simultaneously shaking in their boots and totally hard for some new alien weapons."

Jiang nodded her head slowly. "And this whole innocent-researcher song and dance is a joke," she said, pointing at Vlad. "For one, you're military as hell. That much is obvious. I didn't get to see the rest of your crew before this all went belly up, but I'm betting I'd get the same vibe from them."

Lucky nodded. Vlad was as fit as any fifty-year-old he'd ever seen. And the eye flutters were a dead giveaway for advanced wetwear.

"And this one," Lucky said, pointing at Orton but still speaking to Vlad, "with the desperately obvious over-the-top military hate? He needs acting classes. Badly."

Lucky looked back at Orton. "How are we doing, hotshot?"

Vlad cleared her throat. "Alright, are we done with the guessing game? The point is we don't—"

"Holy hell," said Malby. He was staring upward, eyes unfocused, hands over his head. "We have a problem."

"No kidding," said Cheeky.

"Spit it out, Malby," said Lucky.

"My AI has been monitoring for network activity," he said, talking fast. "We don't have drones up there, but we can put a network together down here and broadcast to see what bounces back."

He was rattled.

"And?" said Lucky.

"And we have nuclear signatures up there in orbit."

"What?" spat Orton, looking up sharply.

Dawson and Jiang jumped to their feet.

"Rocky?"

"I'm reading his feed now," she stated flatly. *"Whatever happened up there is over. They're turning their attention to us."*

This was what Lucky had been afraid of. It was open season on them down here without support above.

"How long?" asked Lucky.

"There are hundreds of signatures," Rocky noted unhelpfully.

The scientists looked bewildered.

"How long until what?" asked Orton.

"Ten minutes until the first impacts. More or less."

Lucky stood up and put his hand on the butt of his pulse rifle. "Until you die in a nuclear fireball," he said.

Orton's face blanched.

It made Lucky's day.

[21]
DIG IN

"Dig in or dust off?" said Jiang.

Spoken like a true Frontier Marine—*right out of the manual,* thought Lucky.

Orbital bombardment was something they trained for. The options were simple; find a deep enough hole to ride it out, or find a way to get airborne. Anything but standing still.

But their options here were limited.

"Dust off is a no-go," said Lucky. "There are Union ships at the mining platforms, but we'd never make it."

Dig in it is, he thought.

"I know this is Union tech, but do you have any AI access?" he asked Rocky. *"Any schematics, anything?"*

He knew it was a long shot. There would be no reason to build a bunker under the stackshack, and at any rate, it would be much too shallow.

"No-go," replied Rocky. Lucky could practically see her shaking her head in frustration. *"There is very little networking to begin with, and what there is just is Union gibberish."*

Lucky looked over at Orton, who was still in shock. His equipment was interpreting Union data. "Is there anything here, like a bunker or underground base, that we can get to in five minutes?"

Orton just stared, but Vlad answered for him.

"Nothing like that, no. This is strictly an excavation site. We detected Union military buildup a few days before we arrived, but nothing more than basic field structures," she said, nodding to the stackshack. "There is nothing deep or permanent here as far as we know."

"We're screwed," said Malby.

"We can go into the crater," offered Jiang.

"It won't give any cover," said Dawson. His happy smile was gone. He was rubbing his wrist.

"It's better than nothing," she snapped.

"It could buy us some time if we don't take a direct hit," said Cheeky.

"You think they don't know exactly where we are?" asked Lucky.

"What about that relic thingy? The spaceship," said Malby. "You said it was made of rock."

"I said it was encrusted in rock," Vlad replied. "It's actually some ore from off-planet. We don't know what it is, exactly. I didn't say it could survive a nuke."

"I thought that ore was everywhere around here."

"That's what I meant," Vlad said absentmindedly.

It didn't sound like what she meant.

But Vlad looked up sharply and snapped her fingers.

"It already has."

"What already has what?" asked Lucky, bewildered.

"This is taking too long," barked Jiang, urgency in her voice.

"You think?" asked Malby. He was near panic.

"When those things attacked, the first time," said Vlad, speaking fast and nodding to herself. "It was when our clone team went to inspect the anomaly. Orton and I stayed up here. We watched the whole ... fight, from here. One of your Marines detonated a field nuke."

"A field nuke? That hardly compares to the ordnance we have inbound," said Lucky.

"No. But the nuke. It didn't scratch the anomaly. Didn't even chip the ore. I remember because I was so worried about the anomaly when we saw the blast from here. It threw the rovers all over the field, scattered them everywhere. But the anomaly..." she shrugged.

Lucky looked around. They were all looking at him.

"Our hero," said Rocky.

"What do you think?" he fired back, ignoring her jab.

"I don't have a better idea. And I'm pretty sure you don't either."

"It'll have to do," he said. "How far?"

"A half klick, but we have to go over the ridge of the crater." She paused. "And through those things," she said, motioning outside.

"That's cutting it close. Let's move, Marines. Combat formations, drones out."

Lucky started for the blast doors, where Cheeky and Jiang already had their rifles out.

"We could dust off," said Nico.

Lucky didn't stop. "How do you figure?"

"We could use the drones," Nico mumbled. "We did that in basic."

Lucky remembered that game. Four or five Marines would marshal all their locusts together and drag one of the rookies kicking and screaming into the air. Lucky could imagine Nico getting persecuted by that little number.

Fun for what it was, but they had lost most of their locusts already, and they needed to do better than getting one Marine a few hundred feet in the air.

Then again.

He turned to Orton. "You said the other Marines were in here?"

Orton nodded. "They set up the camp outside. They had a specialist with a backpack and he opened the blast doors, then they walked through the whole building. It was completely empty. We suspect everyone inside got the same Trojan."

Lucky looked at Jiang.

The others were heading for the door, but she had stopped, already grasping what Lucky was getting at.

"They won't be able to carry us very far," she said, shaking her head.

"Don't have to. Just over the lip of the crater. It won't be pretty, but it will be fast."

Jiang shook her head again, but with less conviction. "Maybe."

Lucky shrugged. "*Maybe* has gotten me out of worse."

"Change of plans!" he yelled. The Marines stopped and turned.

"We're headed to the roof," Lucky said.

"Malby, get your kit," Jiang said. "Time to earn your technical specialist badge."

Lucky nodded at Nico. "You can thank our rookie if this works."

[22]
GIDDY UP

LUCKY BURST through the roof blast doors and took a deep breath. Then he looked up.

He squinted, imagining he could see the nuclear packages whistling through the thin atmosphere, their guidance systems making tiny adjustments to their glide paths.

Not much different from our own approach here less than an hour ago, he thought.

"Malby!" he yelled. "Where's our ride?"

"Gimme a second," Malby said. He was sweating profusely as he worked over his hot box. It was a small gel pack that his AI coordinated with. Lucky didn't understand it, but he knew all technical specialists carried them and they afforded them the ability to do all the fun things they did. "These aren't designed to work like this."

"We'll be dead in two minutes, so no pressure."

"Look out!" Nico shouted as he jumped back from the roof edge.

A pair of cannon barrels the size of Nico's head silently rose to eye level. Wave thrusters rippled the air as it gently rotated to face the roof.

A moment later, another set of barrels came up to the same level beside it.

It was the two stingray rail-gun drones that the landing party had brought with them. The twin rail-guns were mounted to the bottom of a rectangular platform. The topside of the platform wasn't smooth. It had two handholds and an access panel, but it clearly wasn't made for riding on either. "No Step" was stenciled in two places along the platform.

"I'll be damned," Lucky said under his breath.

"This should be fun," echoed Rocky.

Lucky slapped Malby on the back. "Do you have control?"

Malby looked uneasy. The gel back of the hot box was glowing green in his hand, currents flowing through his fingers and into his nanobots.

"I can tell them where to go. I can't explain to them we'll be along for the ride. It might be choppy."

"Understood."

"The rookie and I will take the brainiacs," he said, motioning to the scientists. "Jiang, the Marines are with you."

Vlad looked dubious. Orton, standing behind her, looked sick.

But Lucky took Vlad by the arm and guided her over to one of the stingrays.

"Why can't they just land on the roof?"

"We'll never take off. These things can't support one person's weight, let alone four."

Now Vlad stopped. "So how will we make it?"

"We are forty meters up," Lucky said. He nodded over the roof of the building. "We are one-hundred-fifty meters from the lip of the crater. We just have to get over that lip."

"And after that?"

"After that, we keep falling." Lucky looked at Malby, who shrugged. "Hopefully at a slightly slower pace."

Cheeky and Dawson shared a glance.

"Giddy up," said Cheeky, lips curled in a wicked grin.

Jiang, Malby, Cheeky and Dawson formed a V-shape at the roof's edge in front of their stingray.

"Any activity down there?" Lucky asked Rocky.

"Not yet."

Vlad was at the roof edge now, holding Orton's hand. All his bravado was gone, and Lucky got the impression that the only way he would jump was with Vlad pulling him.

Lucky put his arm on Vlad's shoulder and nodded over at Nico, who did the same with Orton.

Lucky took one last look at the sky and nodded at Jiang.

Jiang nodded back and yelled, "Oohrah!"

The other three Marines answered with a scream of their own, and all four leapt in unison onto the stingray.

Lucky wanted to watch, to see what happened, to gauge his own actions based on how their jump turned out.

But that was pointless. They were jumping either way.

"Go!" he yelled as his grip tightened around Vlad's arm. She hesitated for a second, but Lucky yanked her off her feet and into the air.

Nico yelled as well and did the same with Orton.

He hit the stingray platform and felt it immediately give way, sliding at an angle for a moment before Nico and Orton hit it too.

He leaned forward as the drone began to spin around like a top, swinging wildly from side to side.

Vlad shoved her hand in one of the handholds, but Lucky wasn't so fortunate.

He laid his body as flat as possible, trying to get as much friction on the smooth surface as he could.

The stingray's rudimentary AI adjusted for the imbalance, and Lucky found himself sliding back toward the center of the platform. He and Orton collided headfirst, and Orton began slipping back off the edge.

Lucky grabbed a handful of his hair with one hand and wrapped his other arm around the access box in the center of the platform.

Nico finally got purchase on the other handhold and reached over to put his hand around Orton's waist.

"I got him!" Nico screamed in his face.

Then the stingray plummeted several meters, leaving all four of them swinging upward in the air before crashing back down onto the platform.

What the hell was—

"Damn," Rocky said urgently. *"Multiple contacts!"*

A flurry of blue energy beams flew past the stingray. His spiders were bouncing around, but for once he ignored them.

"They're coordinating their shots."

A thought flashed at Lucky. The eggheads had been right.

They were being controlled from a central point.

[23]
OVER THE EDGE

THE STINGRAY LURCHED at a steep angle, quickly losing altitude. It was angling to fire its big guns.

"Malby!" Lucky screamed into his all-comm. He didn't know where the Marine was or where the other stingray was. "Get us moving!"

"We are!" Malby screamed back.

Lucky glanced up to see the second stingray just above and to the left of their own. He could only see a pair of legs hanging off one end that looked like Dawson.

Malby's disembodied voice continued. "I can only give them the destination ... I can't alter their specific maneuvering!"

The stingray cannon rumbled and the platform lurched as it fired. A moment later, a pair of rovers was lifted partially off the ground in an eruption of dirt.

The maneuver cost them altitude. He felt the stingray pull its nose up, its rudimentary AI adjusting to its sluggish flight path. But they were dangerously low now.

Another stream of blue energy flashed past the platform.

Lying on top, Lucky was blind to the fire coming from below. He heard a pop and grunt from above him and looked up to see a huge hole rip open in the stingray platform the Marines rode on. It swayed, and another pair of legs swung wildly off the side.

"Grab my hand," said Jiang.

"Cheeky, grab his—"

A loud crack was followed by a second pop, and an entire corner of the platform gave way.

As the edge swung downward, Lucky saw Malby claw desperately at the edge of the platform.

His fingers got purchase on the access panel door. Then a third crack, and the panel door came free and Malby fell back with the access door still in his hand.

"Hot box!" shouted Rocky desperately in his head.

Without Malby they couldn't override the rail-gun drones, and there was no telling what they'd do. They certainly wouldn't continue over the lip of the crater and down to the base of the artifact.

"Catch me!" he fired back at Rocky.

He lunged from the edge of the platform. Malby was falling backward and upside down. Lucky reached out for anything he could grab and felt the cool metal of Malby's combat gear on his fingertips but knew he wouldn't be able to hold him. Malby was a goner. He'd never get him.

And then something smashed into his hand, and he clamped down with all his strength.

He looked upward—which was straight down now—to see Malby's combat boot in his hand. In the same instant, he felt his own foot yanked backward.

He looked back to see one of Rocky's drones wedging his boot into the barrel of one of the giant rail-gun cannons. As he watched, two more locust drones slammed into their cousin, totally lodging his boot into the giant muzzle.

"Really?"

He hung upside down with his foot wedged in the business end of a cannon.

"Best I could do on short notice," said Rocky.

He glanced back at Malby who stared up at him with wild eyes.

"Keep that hot box hot, Malby. We're almost there."

"I don't fucking care!"

Fair point.

Lucky didn't feel that optimistic, his lack of optimism matched by the dwindling distance to the rovers below.

And then he felt a warming sensation in his boot.

The rail-gun was about to fire.

"Rocky!"

He looked back down to Malby. "Malby!"

Screaming names didn't actually seem to be helping, but he was running thin on ideas.

Then he heard his own name.

"Lucky!"

He looked up to see Nico, who had crawled under the platform and was hanging from the rail-gun, hand extended.

In one motion, Lucky grabbed his wrist and rotated his body to release his boot from the rail-gun that was about to fire.

Swinging back, he watched as the three locusts that had lodged his foot swung below him to give Malby a boost, who was treating Lucky's outstretched hand like a rope ladder, clawing his way up.

The stingray fired, a hot blast washing over Lucky's face. The platform shuddered, and a shaft of blue light flared up from the ground below him.

And then something hard smashed into his leg, which was dangling now that he'd swung around to put his weight on Nico.

The top of a rover had smashed every bone in his leg.

He swung wildly, and for a moment thought he might pull Nico down with him, but he saw Malby struggling for purchase on the bottom of the rail-gun. He had the hot box between his teeth.

Lucky sacrificed the last of his balance to shove his boot as far up Malby's ass as possible, hoping it hurt, pushing the Marine the last few feet up the side of the stingray platform. The inertia pushed Lucky straight toward the ground, which was rising fast.

He hit it, rolled, and watched as Malby, Nico and the stingray slid over the crater edge with inches to spare.

Lucky felt his spiders clawing at his mind, felt a pluck and swung to his left as a blue stream darted past his head.

He turned to find four of the Union puppets advancing on his position.

In another time and place, it might have been a nice family portrait. A middle-aged man in a jumpsuit, a slightly older woman in overalls, and two girls in jumpers.

Unfortunately, they were all missing eyes. And they all held weapons at their hips and pointed them at Lucky.

But other than that, a real nice moment.

The nearest girl fired, but a locust appeared from the heavens, diving into the shot and disintegrating.

Another followed it, smashing into the girl and folding her in half, sending her weapon flying.

Lucky began to hop backward, dragging his broken leg with him and considering his options. The stimulants his biobots fed him dulled the pain, but didn't help with the uselessness of the leg, which was minutes from regeneration.

He saw a rover to his right and considered running for the open cab. Or hopping. He also knew it likely contained yet another of these things. Maybe he could get the drop on it.

And then the ground disappeared below him.

He was falling, bouncing with bone-crushing intensity.

He had backed right over the edge of the crater.

[24]
ALMOST

He rolled to a stop.

He couldn't feel his legs. He couldn't feel his hands.

He couldn't feel anything.

"Rocky, what's the story here?"

Nothing.

"Rocky?"

"Bad news."

"I got that. How bad?"

"Broken back. Two minutes."

Lucky raised his head. He had limited neck movement, but nothing from the shoulders down. He knew even as his mind raced that his biobots were working furiously to fuse together the nerve damage in his back, reconnecting tissues in ways science could never have done a century ago.

But two minutes was going to get him killed.

The alien ship was still another hundred yards away, and there were even more of the rovers crammed around here. If it wasn't obvious before, the artifact was undoubtedly the main attraction drawing all of thesc things to it.

He watched as the stingray carrying his Marines

smashed into the ground, spilling them at the base of the anomaly.

"At least someone is making progress," said Rocky.

"Can we call them?"

"Done. Now what? They can't get here any faster than you can get there. And there are lots of—"

Lucky was watching for the second stingray when a pair of skinny, wrinkled ankles dropped into his line of sight. An elderly woman in muddy pants had crawled slowly from the passenger side of the rover to his right. She walked purposefully toward him.

"Rocky?"

"Another minute."

He strained at his arms, willing them to work. His rifle lay tantalizingly close, right across the palm of his hand. He could see his hand. See his finger. See the trigger. But nothing he could do could put the two of them together.

He looked back at the old woman, her face now obscured by the weapon she held aloft. For the second time today, Lucky was staring right down the barrel.

He gritted his teeth.

Not like this.

He was no hero, certainly not like his sister. He wasn't worth a damn. He wasn't worth having his name said in hushed tones while no one remembered her.

But he was worth more than this. Worth more than being killed by a senior citizen with a blaster that was smaller than her shrunken head.

What makes you think you deserve better?

That wasn't Rocky. It hadn't come through his echo channel. It was something else, something deeper, something that knew him more intimately than he knew himself.

The voice had a lilt to it, a twinkle in the words. There was a smile behind the words, a laugh.

It was the voice of madness, Lucky realized.

It was Him.

"Rocky?"

No response.

He felt his finger twitch. Could he get to the trigger of his gun?

Maybe he could lift the gun, kill the old woman, make a run for the anomaly. Maybe he could get back control. Maybe he could stop it.

But he couldn't.

Red clouds billowed up in his vision, swirling around faster and faster.

He felt himself start to laugh. A big, booming laugh. A playful laugh, like a child full of wonder.

The woman faltered. She tilted her head. Hair fell across the red crusted scars on her blind face.

She closed the gap, never lowering her weapon, never wavering. But not firing either. She came closer and closer as the wild, childish laughter grew louder and louder until Lucky couldn't recognize it as his own voice any longer.

She came until the metal of her gun kissed the polymer of his faceplate.

And suddenly, the laughter stopped, and Lucky felt the rage turn on in a blinding rush.

His head smashed forward with such violence it snapped the gun sideways and the woman lost her grip.

He watched as his own arm came up with his weapon in hand, and in one motion his other hand grabbed the back of the old woman's head and bent her in half over the rifle, then watched as the pulse punch of the gun ripped her frail body in half.

A far-off voice was yelling and screaming, like there was struggle. But it was so, so far away.

He could barely hear it, barely make anything out. What was it saying?

He strained, but it was unintelligible.

Then he heard his own voice howl in rage.

In an instant, he was leaping toward another eyeless puppet, this one an older man with sunken cheeks. He hadn't gotten out of the rover yet, hadn't even had time to lift his weapon.

Lucky leapt into the cab with him.

He saw his pulse rifle flash, heard himself laugh again.

The Hate was so very happy, like a prisoner released from his cell.

But this time the far-off voice was closer, more determined. Stronger.

"Lucky!" it screamed.

He recognized it. He knew that voice. He had heard it before, but his mind refused to work. It was fuzzy with rage.

He was over the man now, crushing him on the floorboard of the cab, beating him with something.

"Lucky!" came the voice in his head again, more urgent this time.

"Lucky, we're regen'd up. You don't need this."

Now he was sure he recognized the voice.

Another swing, and the eyeless face sank inward. The head splattered.

And then all the animosity in his mind simply drained away.

Until next time, Lucky.

It was the dark voice from somewhere else in his mind. But it was weak and distant.

The red clouds in his vision burned away. He could think clearly.

"Okay, I got it now. He's back in the bottle. I got Him, Lucky. I got Him."

"He got out?"

"Just for a minute, but we're okay now."

Lucky looked down at the destroyed, crumpled face and body of the eyeless man.

He dropped what he'd been hitting him with. A ragged leg ripped off at the knee joint. The man's own leg.

"You know it could've been worse," Rocky said.

Lucky glanced out of the front cab and realized it *was* worse. Much worse.

An eyeless was right next to the cab's window. Two more lie only a dozen steps away.

He looked down at the destroyed eyeless man on the floorboard, then up at the display column.

Aw, hell.

He grabbed the man's bloody head and slammed it up next to the AI sensor, hoping there was enough brain activity still going on in there for the rover to recognize the link with its owner and—

The rover's engine roared to life.

He slammed the power column forward, and it lurched ahead.

Lucky sat up and reached for the steering column. There was nothing there. He looked down. Nothing.

What kind of backward, ignorant, AI-stupid people build a rover with a physical control column for thrust and not one for steering?

The Union, that's who.

"Rocky, I got a little problem."

"Don't look at me. I can't interface with this Union gobbledygook."

"So how do I steer?"

"I don't know, but you'd better figure it out."

He felt the rover smash up against another one parked at a different angle, which threw his in a new direction. At least the crazy motion of his drive made him a difficult target.

But it was also sending him the wrong way. He was driving parallel to the alien ship, and the longer he drove without turning, the larger a course alteration he would need.

A blue energy beam flew wildly over the rover, then another scorched the dirt next to his big front tire.

That gave him an idea.

He jumped over to the passenger door of the cab, kicked it open, and swung his head out. He pulled his punch pistol from his shoulder holster and fired one punch into the big tire.

It exploded with a bang, and the rover started listing to the right.

Lucky's spiders plucked urgently, and he swung up just as a blue energy beam lanced down the side of the cab where his head had been. He looked back to find an ugly man with fat arms hanging out of the back of the rover bed.

As he watched, three more eyeless clambered out.

Of course, he thought.

He pulled himself back inside in time to see they were headed for a collision with three rovers parked in a semicircle. He was going to hit the center rover head on.

He leaned down to brace for impact and saw the dead eyeless man's blaster.

He grabbed it and fired through the front view of the

rover. It sliced through the metal like it wasn't there and blew a perfect line down the center of the rover dead ahead of him.

The energy beam caused the rover to break apart into two similarly sized chunks. It didn't, however, clear his path. One side rolled away, but the other fell right into his path.

His rover hit it with the flat right tire and bounced up and over the debris, leaping skyward. For a moment he was weightless, then gravity reasserted itself and slammed the rover back down.

It bounced, swinging wildly on the flat front tire, then flipped up on its nose and stood upright, teetering for a full second, then toppled over onto its roof.

Lucky rolled out. With the Union blaster in hand, he sliced again and again through the back bed of the rover where the other eyeless had been. Then he pulled out his own rifle, flipped it, and launched a pulse grenade, then flipped it back and dived away.

The rover, or at least what was left of it, exploded in a fireball.

Lucky turned to run.

And looked straight into Malby's face.

Jiang and Dawson stood next to him.

He looked up to see he was standing at the base of the alien ship.

"Hey," he said. "Sorry I took so long."

[25]
HOME

Beams of blue energy shot overhead, glancing off the anomaly without leaving a scratch.

That shit was tough, whatever it was.

The Marines scattered. Jiang fired two pulses, and Lucky saw one of the eyeless crumple.

Malby started back toward the anomaly, rifle up.

"Holy hell, Lucky," he said. "You do know how to make an entrance."

Dawson fired off two pulses at another eyeless.

"Coolest thing I've seen in a long time," Cheeky said as the Marines reformed and fell back together in a carefully defensive formation.

"Should I tell them you nearly pissed yourself, or will you?" Rocky asked.

Something exploded overhead, and for a moment he thought they'd taken too long. But it was just a stingray with a broken platform spinning lazily, firing its twin cannons into the maze of rovers.

The other stingray was on the ground, apparently too damaged from the hard landing to lift off again.

The Marines had formed defensive positions around the base of a sheer wall of gray ore that reached up at least fifteen meters. It was smooth, offering no easy ascent.

"Where are our scientists?" said Rocky.

Good question. The brain gang was nowhere in sight.

"Where could they've gone?"

"The locusts can't get bearings on anything near that ore."

Malby was staring over Lucky's shoulder. He turned, expecting to see another eyeless Unionite, but instead saw a mushroom cloud in the distance.

"What're we waiting for?" asked Lucky.

"A way in," said Jiang.

Vlad's voice surprised them all. "Let's go! This way!"

She was motioning around a second rock formation with identical sheer cut sides. But the ground beyond was grooved with angular sides that seemed to climb up subtly.

Lucky was sure it hadn't been there a moment before. But how could that be? The rock formations looked ancient. This hadn't been disturbed in eons.

They all ran around the corner, then stopped.

Three Marine bodies were slumped on the ground.

One was splayed at an angle, with most of her head split down the middle, her faceplate crushed and mangled.

Another nearby had massive wounds that could only have come from an Empire high-impact grenade. He must have taken a hit and gone into regen with it in his hand.

The Marine next to him had massive damage to the back of his head.

One grenade, two unlucky Marines.

"Where are the rest?" asked Malby as he ran to the nearest dead Marine and started to rip out pulse recharger pods. He tossed one to Jiang who slapped it to her gear pack.

"Nuke blast on the east side," said Jiang. "Saw it as we landed."

Cheeky was nodding next to her. "They blew themselves and a half-mile radius of these bastards to hell."

Dawson was scavenging one of the other Marines, straining to avoid disturbing the pulped-up face. He threw a couple charge pods to Lucky. He tossed one to Nico. The kid looked shocked.

"Get over it," Lucky said. "We need 'em more than they do."

The ground around them started to rumble.

"What's that?" asked Nico.

"Oh hell," whined Malby.

"Let's move," barked Jiang.

The ground bounced violently now, and for the first time Lucky sensed a difference in the look and feel of the artifact and the ground below it. The vibrations made the whole thing suddenly come into focus. The scale was so massive it hadn't registered from where they were.

They weren't on the ground anymore.

They were on an artificial deck. Inside the ship.

Lucky still couldn't understand how they had even entered the ship. There was something maddeningly fluid about it, like the walls were shifting around them. And yet. Everything still looked like ancient, unchanging rock. Damned peculiar.

They slipped under a ledge of flat gray rock and climbed up one more steep incline. The twisting path meant Lucky could look back and see nothing but ancient rock. But had they gone that far? Now he wasn't so sure. And the angle of the approach seemed wrong. They had scaled a steep incline, but the path behind now seemed too shallow.

Perspective was hard to judge within the walls of sheer gray rock. *Maybe it's playing tricks on my mind?*

"Do we have a better plan than just to go as deep into this thing as we can?" he shouted upward.

No answer from the scientists, who were already up top.

He doubted anyone heard him. The rumbling was louder now.

"Ummmm," Rocky started. *"So, here's a thing."*

"A thing?"

"Well ... ummmm."

Only my AI could get tongue-tied, Lucky mused.

Dawson stood at one side of a steep ledge, helping Nico crawl up. Cheeky was doing the same for Jiang.

Lucky saw Malby reaching over the edge.

"Gimme your hand!" he screamed. The vibration of the rock ore around them was deafening. It felt as if it might break apart at any moment.

But then Lucky's mind froze.

Over Malby's shoulder, inside the cavernous space that the scientists and Marines were scrambling across, were symbols.

Alien symbols.

Alien symbols that Lucky had seen before in his nightmares. And here they were, just as he had left them in his dreams, embedded in the rock walls around him.

Malby was screaming at him now, right in his face. But Lucky couldn't hear him.

Rocky echoed out something, but it too was drowned out. Something loud and high-pitched resonated in his ears.

He could read the symbols. And so could He.

Welcome home, Lucky, said The Hate.

And then the ground vibrated one last time, and he was thrown into the air like a scarecrow in tornado alley.

Everything went black.

[26]
SPECIMEN

HELLO, nightmare.

Hello, Lucky, said his nightmare.

Lucky woke up and just wanted to breathe.

He was drowning. Green-yellow liquid covered his face, filling his eyes, his nose, his mouth.

He tried to reach up, but his hands wouldn't move.

He tried to yell, but his mouth wouldn't open.

He was frozen inside a tank of gel, staring upward into a vast open space.

A head hovered over him.

A machine head.

A phalanx of metal tubes protruded from the face. There were no eyes, no nose, no mouth. Only the tubes. There was a glass lens in each, and as the head moved closer Lucky could see his own sickly visage reflected in each one of the tubes.

The package of tubes spun wildly with a high-pitched

whine, and a green light grew in a central point just below them.

The glow grew until Lucky could see there were images now there. Some alien terrain he couldn't understand. A barren, folded landscape. Alien symbols were overlaid on the map, highlighting sections that turned blue and green.

"It's not working," said a disembodied voice he realized was coming from the machine face. And then it dawned on him it wasn't just a machine. This was a human, but so heavily modified it was beyond recognition.

It reached an arm over Lucky, and he saw a curved set of metal prods with a fine electric line running between them, like a tiny bit of floss. It dipped silently into the terrain projected in front of the metal tubes. It disappeared into the green, and then there was the slightest twitch of the hand.

Lucky felt incredible pain from somewhere deep inside his brain.

He screamed, or tried to, but nothing came out.

He felt excruciating, bone-jarring pain fire up and down his body, attacking his brain over and over again, like a war going on inside of him.

The arm of the man pulled back from the image in front of the tubes, and Lucky felt the pain in his mind subside.

The alien terrain was his mind. They were doing something to his mind.

"It *is* working," came a mild reply. This was also disembodied, but much closer to his face.

Another person stepped into view, his head also silhouetted by the bright light above him. A human. A normal human.

He wore a black uniform with brown insignias across the left shoulder.

His cheeks were hollow, and his eyes were inset. It didn't look like he had eaten in many days. His eyes were bloodshot.

"His body is rejecting it, just like the others," said the machine face. His voice was deep and angry.

"That doesn't mean it isn't working. It will take time."

"We don't have time. She is waiting."

"He shows the most promise of any of the specimens. I told you when this started there was a seeding process, did I not?"

"And I told you she is not patient. If you cannot give me breakthroughs, you must give me advances."

There was a pause, and then the tubes abruptly stopped their swirling. The floating green images faded and disappeared.

"If we stop now, it will overwhelm him. Like the others."

"Better to kill him than to kill us."

There was a pause.

"She will kill you. Not us."

And then Lucky felt something float through his mind. It was a red flash of color at the edges of his vision.

It poked in his mind, behind his eyes. He felt the sensation of a twitch on his face.

For a moment, the man with the metal tubes looked down at Lucky. The tubes didn't spin, but they shifted. One tube slid over, then another, then another.

Then he looked away again.

And the red cloud floated through his mind again. Lucky could feel it. Pure, blind hate.

You are needed, said The Hate.

And then a voice whispered harshly in his ear. "*Your nightmare is just starting.*"

[27]
DUST OFF

LUCKY JERKED HIS HEAD UPRIGHT, crashing into the faceplate of Nico leaning over him, and felt his head bang back down.

"Lucky!" said Nico, falling back. "You okay?"

He felt his head bounce hard against the ground again. And again. He couldn't stop the rattling. His teeth shook, his head shook, his everything shook.

"Stop shaking me, asshole," he growled.

Nico looked over his shoulder, then back at Lucky. He wasn't shaking him. Everything around him was shaking him.

"How long—"

"You passed out as we were climbing up. Malby grabbed you."

Great, now he owed the little asshole.

"What the hell is going on?"

Dawson and Cheeky were bracing themselves against a wall of gray ore. The composition was similar to the rock that seemed to be draped over the outside of the alien ship.

It struck him that the gray ore wasn't draped over the

ship. It *was* the ship. Maybe he already knew that. Or maybe the scientists did. But he hadn't really believed it until this moment.

How can a ship be made entirely of rock?

He reached out to the vibrating rock wall beside him. The composition seemed to be overlocking sheets of this banded gray ore. They were fused together, but in such a way that the bands of darker colors that permeated them seemed to flow from one sheet of ore to the next. As if the ore had grown together naturally.

The cavernous space they were in was enormous, at least five-hundred meters in each direction and twice that in height, Lucky guessed. Several pathways led away from it that looked almost like caves thanks to the gray rock composition of the walls.

It was also empty.

At the far end, near the recessed script, were a half-dozen grooved arches spaced evenly across the sheer rock. He glanced at the alien script and sensed they were something like access points to allow whatever was supposed to fit in here easy entry and egress.

How did I know that? Just an educated guess, he told himself.

But it was more than that. Looking at the script had seeded the idea in his mind.

He started to ask Rocky when she echoed him.

"There has been an ... incident."

"You don't say?" he replied sarcastically.

Rocky didn't take the bait.

He surveyed the room. Orton and Vlad were huddled together whispering harshly.

"Well, I just had another experiment nightmare. And it was triggered by this ship."

"You think the experiment was here?"

Lucky looked around.

"No, the symbols are wrong, and the space was even bigger," he echoed. *"But it's related. Closely related."*

"Yeah. I think the ship knows us. Or me."

What did that—

Before he could respond, Malby lunged at Orton.

"You said it wasn't possible!" he screamed, pinning the scientist to the ground.

"It isn't possible!" rasped Orton.

Jiang and Cheeky were beside Nico.

Lucky was still sitting.

Once again it was left to Dawson to step in and pull Malby back.

Lucky stood shakily, the rumble almost gone now.

"What's the situation out there?"

No one said anything.

"The nukes. Are the nukes hitting yet? Will this thing hold up?"

Jiang said, "That's not the concern at the moment."

He stared at her incredulously. "Oh?"

"You've been ... out for a few minutes," she said, looking at him pointedly again. Lucky was sure he'd jumped with her before. She had his number.

Finally, Malby spoke. "We're no longer on the surface of the planet."

Lucky whipped his head around so fast it hurt. "What?"

The room was silent. He glanced from face to face.

Orton's wasn't beet red for once. It was white as a sheet.

Vlad was staring directly at him. The intensity of the gaze suggested more than a passing glance, but he couldn't read her expression.

He was about to ask Malby how he knew, then realized

the tech specialist was still the only one with some drone net access. He probably had a front-and-center view of—

Of what? Of the multi-billion-year-old ship taking off?

Impossible.

"How—"

"Beats me. But we have positive pressure in here. It's sealed up."

"What's propelling us? Did the aliens leave the tanks half full or something?"

Malby waved in his face. "Hello, asshole. I'm in here with you, idiot. How should I know? That's what I'm asking the brain trust back here." He hooked a thumb back at Orton.

The pudgy scientist just shook his head and mumbled to himself.

Then Rocky told him.

"I'm flying the ship, Lucky."

[28]

IN CHARGE

"*YOU'RE DOING WHAT?*"

The shock must have registered on his face.

Vlad pointed at Lucky. "It's you," she said calmly.

All heads swiveled to look at him.

"I didn't say anything about it back there because I didn't see any point in alarming anyone. But when the original landing party got here, they couldn't figure out how to get in. I knew there would be a way. There always is. But I didn't know how fast we'd be able to find it."

Lucky realized what she was saying.

"That ramp. It wasn't there when the first landing party came here?"

She nodded. "And it wasn't there when we first got dumped off those ridiculous drones," she said, motioning skyward. "But it was there when you got here."

Lucky said, "When we all got here."

But it was true. He *had* arrived a full minute after the rest of the Marines.

"You two were nowhere to be found when I got here," he shot back. "What's to say you didn't trigger it somehow?

You know,"—he waved his arms—"lean on a lever or something."

Orton rolled his eyes.

Lucky scowled at him. "Well, it's either that, or I'm alien magic."

The Marines looked at each, clearly now uncomfortable.

"Guys? Seriously? Alien magic?" He laughed, holding his hands up in a shrug.

No one else moved or spoke.

"So am I alien magic?" he asked Rocky. *"Or are you?"*

"A little of both, I think."

This was the point where jumping with a totally different division on the opposite side of the galaxy was not working in his favor.

Finally, Dawson laughed. "This fucker is a lot of things, but he's no ship driver. I mean, no offense, but has your AI ever run anything bigger than drones?"

Vlad walked toward him.

Lucky kept his face a mask. He was a decent poker player.

She stopped inches from his face. Her breath was warm on his lips. "As soon as you got here, you passed out and this ship came to life. That is a hell of a coincidence," she said.

"We have a problem," said Rocky.

"You mean, other than this bitch in my grill and my AI piloting an ancient alien starship?"

"Yes." She hesitated. *"My understanding is that we are exposed to the nukes as we ascend."*

"It's your understanding?"

There was a pregnant pause. *"The ship told me different."*

Lucky worked overtime on his poker face. Vlad wasn't backing down.

He turned over Rocky's statement. It was one thing to say she was flying the ship; it was another to be talking to it.

"So there is an AI on board."

"Something like an AI."

"And you're talking to it."

"Easily, yes."

"You can't even jack into Union AI traffic without a workaround, but you're telling me you can just interact with the AI system on a ship that is, what, eight-billion-years-old? And why couldn't Vlad and her team just jack in the same way?"

"I don't know."

Lucky exhaled. He hadn't realized he was holding his breath. It probably smelled like shit because Vlad stepped back.

He looked around at the others. Despite Dawson's words, he could tell the room wasn't with him.

"I'm going to tell them."

"Do you think that's a good idea?"

"Do you have a better one?"

Lucky looked at Vlad. "You have it wrong. I'm not in charge." He glanced at Jiang. "My AI is."

[29]
T'KET'KA

JIANG GASPED.

"Bullshit," said Malby.

"I'm not going to explain how, because frankly, I don't understand how. And I don't think Rocky does either."

It was strange to say the name of his AI aloud. It wasn't something he ever did, or ever heard other augmented Marines do. They would mention their AI copilot in terms of assistance in combat, but beyond that, it wasn't something that came up in ordinary situations.

As if reading his mind, Malby said, "Who?"

"My AI."

"You named your AI Rocky?"

It sounded even weirder when Malby said it.

"I'm not a pet! I wasn't named!" Rocky insisted.

Lucky knew he had an unusual situation with Rocky. But since he spoke of it so seldom, he didn't know just how unusual.

"What's yours named?"

Malby looked incredulous. "It doesn't have a freaking name! It's my AI. It controls my drones. It feeds me data dumps. It overlays the combat theater. I don't have chats with it over beer."

"His loss," said Rocky.

"Can we not do this now?" said Jiang. "I don't care what you call your AI. If it *is* in control, as you say, then where exactly are we going?"

"Good question," he shot to Rocky.

"Not sure," she volleyed back.

"That might not go over well with the peanut gallery here."

Vlad was right back in Lucky's grill, and he still wasn't liking that one bit.

"Hang on," Rocky said.

"What is that supposed to—"

Suddenly the floor shifted dramatically under them. For a split second they all were lifted off the ground and the floor tilted at a sharp angle.

Something in the gravity altered wildly around them, and they were all swung over to match the floor. And then it was level again.

Lucky felt the pit of his stomach jump and stretch. He held back vomit that welled up in his throat.

Orton made no such effort and blew chunks all over Nico, which seemed appropriate.

"We can't dodge these nukes as we get higher in the atmosphere. We have to do something."

Lucky sighed. *"For the first time in my life, I wish everyone could hear what you are saying."*

He relayed Rocky's message to Vlad.

In an amazing turn of events, the scientists seemed to have their heads screwed on better than the Marines. Only Jiang had moved past the Rocky revelation.

Vlad frowned and looked back at Orton.

"The T'ket'ka," he said, as if it was obvious.

Vlad's eyes got huge. "But I told you—"

"I know what you said. But—"

A tremor went through the ship.

"Another nuke?"

"No, I think the ship ... I think the ship was reacting to his suggestion."

"I assume it isn't a fan of these T'ket'ka things."

"Quite the opposite. It doesn't want to lose any of them."

Orton was still arguing with Vlad.

"We have more than a dozen," he said. "We can risk one."

"We don't know what it will do! It might kill us all. We might lose everything."

"Whoa!" said Malby, finally emerging from his daze.

"Whoa is right," drawled Dawson. "How might it kill us?"

Orton was exasperated. "It's what we came here for."

"Orton!" said Vlad.

"It's the holy grail," he said, ignoring her. "We're almost sure of it. It seems to be what the Union is building all their new tech around. It's a power source of some kind."

"And it still works?" Jiang asked. "How is that even possible?"

"It's a perpetual energy source. Undamaged, it cannot be depleted. It's one of the only things in the universe we are sure would survive a multi-billion-year hibernation."

He looked at Vlad.

She sighed.

"He's right," she said. "It must be what the Union has. We have hypothesized something like this was out there. We just didn't imagine that the Union would stumble upon it, or know how to use it. We still don't quite understand how they know what to do with it." She motioned outside the ship. "It might be what's behind everything that's happening to them as well."

Orton shook his head. "No, that is from the second anomaly," he said firmly.

This argument was getting old.

Without warning, the ship performed another puke-inducing shift.

Lucky felt as if his internal organs moved a split second after the rest of him. It actually hurt.

Orton puked again. Nico had the good sense not to be next to him this time.

"A little warning, Rocky!"

"Here's a warning. It's going to get worse."

"Bottom line," Lucky said, trying to compose himself. "What we're referring to, is ..."

He glanced between Vlad and Orton expectantly.

Orton wiped puke off his chin. His hands were trembling. "A form of antimatter is probably the easiest way for *you* to think of it."

Even facing death, he was a condescending prick.

"Obviously," said Lucky.

"Dammit," said Malby.

Dawson whistled to himself.

"So we have something"—Lucky shook his head—"anti-matter-ish on board. How does this help us?"

Rocky answered for him. *"We drop it. We destabilize it. We run like hell."*

"But the ship doesn't want you to do it," said Lucky. *"Why?"*

"Beats me. But look, I have drones outside still. Those Union skreamers are going to have a clean shot at us as we

crest the atmosphere. As far as I can tell after talking to this thing, it doesn't have weapons. I'm out of ideas."

Lucky relayed the message to the group.

Orton nodded. He was on the ground and wasn't getting up. "Do it."

Vlad looked like she was going to be sick too, but it wasn't the motion.

Of the two of them, Lucky suspected she was the one with her neck on the line. The Empire had something bad in store for her if she didn't deliver on some weaponizeable tech. That was how the Empire played this game.

"You get that, Rocky? It sounds like you're good to go."

"Oh good," she replied. *"I did it two minutes ago."*

[30]
TROUBLE

"It's dropping with a drone following. It's going to shoot it when we get some distance from it."

"How big is it?" Lucky imagined a huge object composed of the same rock ore as the ship.

Rocky showed him an image of a smooth pearl-white sphere, no more than fifty-centimeters across.

"That's it?"

"That's it," she said. *"The ship AI tells me it should be quite a show."*

Lucky jerked his head up. "Hey, Tech Specialists. You still got orbitals?"

Malby shook his head, then stopped. "Wait, yeah," he said. "Now that we're nearing space, I see maybe,"—he paused, eyes unfocused—"two half-functional. Nothing weaponized."

"Can you get us visuals?"

Malby frowned.

A moment later, Rocky had pumped through the view from Malby's AI to his mind's eye.

Lucky had the same strange out-of-body experience he

always had when using far-range drones to look down on his own position. He could see the alien ship streaking out of the planet's upper atmosphere.

He could also see the massing Union destroyers now in low orbit with the other view. Several squadrons of skreamers were heading their way. They were in the same V-formation they had used to slice their own Empire destroyers into pieces just a few short hours ago.

They were going to be easy pickings out here in orbit, especially if Rocky was right and this old bucket didn't have weapons.

And then something else caught his eye. A pinpoint of light near the planet's surface.

At first he thought it was another nuclear mushroom. More than two dozen were clouding the surface.

Malby grunted. "Some weird reading on that ... on that ..." His voice trailed off.

The pinpoint was expanding with lightning speed.

"That isn't possible," said Malby.

Distance and perspective made even the most dramatic scenes unfold in excruciating slowness from orbit. But not this. It was spreading faster than anything Lucky had ever seen.

"What are we seeing?" Jiang asked.

Wherever the bright flame danced, the planet's surface retreated. It simply ceased to be. Everywhere matter existed, the leaping flame extinguished it. Within seconds, the hemisphere of the planet that had just been below them was gone.

The effect on gravity was turbulence-inducingly immediate. Space shifted and twisted around them, unable to cope with the sudden deforming of matter.

The flame continued onward across the surface of the

planet, but as it did Lucky noticed the color was changing. It was growing redder. And moving closer to the view from the drone.

"It's riding up the atmosphere!" yelled Malby.

Orton turned wide-eyed to Vlad, and for the first time it dawned on Lucky that the scientists couldn't see what the Marines were seeing.

"The antimatter is eating the planet," he said. "It's literally disappearing before our drone eyes. And now it looks like it is eating its way up through the atmosphere."

Orton's face blanched.

Vlad closed her eyes. "Yes," she said quietly. "That makes sense. It will be hungry for matter. It's going to gorge on the planet, but once that is gone it will turn on the particles in the atmosphere. It won't stop until it reaches space."

Lucky didn't like the way she was personifying the antimatter. He liked even less how she seemed to be enjoying the image of it happening.

"And what if we are still in the atmosphere when that happens?"

No one spoke.

"How about it?" he said to Rocky.

"We're clear now. Technically."

"What do you mean, technically?"

"Well, the end of the atmosphere is subjective. There are some lingering particles here in low orbit. If we really want to get to total vacuum, we have to go higher."

"And ..."

"And we need to go higher," agreed Rocky, catching on.

"Bingo."

"Hang on."

The ground shifted harshly once more, and again he felt the floor move and his own body rotate in midair as the gravity struggled to keep up. His stomach twisted in knots again.

Nico looked warily at Orton, but the scientist managed to keep what was left of his lunch down this time.

In his mind's eye the flame was climbing higher, chasing their ship as it burned away from the atmosphere. It dawned on Lucky in that moment that he didn't actually know how the ship was under power.

"It uses the T'ket'ka in a perpetual energy pattern. They feed on a matter loop, and the energy is dispersed as matter and antimatter flip places."

"Sorry I asked. Just tell me we will make it."

Silence.

Finally, he heard Rocky again.

"We're going to make it into space. After that, all bets are off."

In his mind's eye, Lucky watched as the last of the planetoid burned away, simply vanishing, as if nothing had ever been there. Then he realized it was chaos in orbit.

The drone they were using for visuals was spinning about, already losing its bearings without the orbital pull of the planetoid.

The chaos extended to the Union destroyers, who were scrambling to find their bearings.

The skreamers were nowhere to be seen. They'd been skimming at very low orbit and had been caught up in the last of the antimatter reaction and devoured.

A shitty way to go, thought Lucky.

"We got trouble," said Rocky.

The view in his mind's eye now switched to the view from the nose of the ship. Lucky wondered idly how she got that view. Perhaps she had locusts riding shotgun. Perhaps.

Three Union destroyers, safe from the carnage in higher orbit, were bearing down on them.

Cannon pulses poured from their batteries, streaking across the vacuum.

Lucky sighed.

This was a more conventional way to go.

But no less shitty.

"Incoming!" he yelled.

[31]
STUNNED

THE IMAGE in his mind's eye blinked out.

The ship rocked slightly.

The Marines, all in various poses of bracing themselves against whatever they could around them, looked at Lucky quizzically.

"Thanks, I guess," said Malby.

What the hell?

"That was it?" he echoed.

"You were hoping for more?"

"So we're home free? If that is all they have."

"The ore is strong, and those destroyer pulses were from distance and conventional."

"I'm not liking where you're going with this."

"We have more skreamers inbound. We've seen what their ordnance can do. I'm not sure what it can do to us, but I'd rather not stick around to find out."

This time, he didn't see with his mind's eye. He didn't need to.

A light gathered across the banded rock walls, then focused on a point near the base of the alien script they had first passed as they crawled into the cavernous space in the belly of the ship.

An image of space appeared, floating in air, and for an instant Lucky had the sensation of looking at the green terrain of his own mind floating over him from his nightmare.

Now what he saw was the near-space around the ship.

The others gathered around.

"What are we seeing?" Malby asked.

"Rocky?"

"This was an option all along, I just had to ... understand better what was on offer."

"I still can't understand how you can interact."

"I can't either. I didn't have to do a handshake or follow any protocols. I just had access when I looked for it."

Lucky frowned. That was too fortuitous to accept.

"It's the best visual we are going to get in here," he said to Malby and the rest of the group. "Let's call it a ship's eye," he said, improvising.

"Those skreamers are in formation again," said Jiang.

The others had been burned up in low orbit, but these were pouring down from the two destroyers bearing down on them from high orbit.

"Can we outrun them?" Lucky asked, out loud this time for the benefit of the group.

"No," echoed Rocky.

Lucky shook his head.

"Of course not," said Vlad. "This ship isn't built for conventional speed."

"What is it built for?" asked Lucky, suspiciously.

He hadn't forgotten how quick she'd been to turn on him.

"The second anomaly," Vlad said.

Orton looked up sharply.

"This ship is designed to pass through that anomaly," she said, nodding slowly at Orton. "It doesn't need to move fast through space. It can pass through folds in space."

Orton's eyes grew big. "The wormholes. They exist? But we never had anything definitive on that. We lost those operatives years ago." He pursed his lips, his eyebrows drawn down and tight like a petulant child just learning his friends have better toys than him. "Why didn't you share it with the team? How long have you known? What can we—"

Vlad held up a hand. "Is now the time?" she asked, then turned to Lucky.

Orton was left staring at the back of her head.

"We have to get to the second anomaly. It's our only chance to get out of here."

Lucky took a long hard look at Vlad.

Not all military brainiacs were made the same. Some were soft, like Orton. Some were not. Vlad's physique suggested regular exercise and a strict diet. A Marine first.

He swung fast and tight.

As he expected, she instinctively tried to step inside the punch, but he kept the swing compact. He caught her just in front of the ear. It was a glancing blow that should have just stunned her.

At least, that was what he was going for.

Vlad crumpled to the floor.

[32]
CLEVER

"Damn," said Malby, eyebrows raised.

"You piece of shit!" yelled Orton, rushing over to Vlad.

He glared at Lucky with an expression he probably thought was menacing.

Lucky rested his palm on his rifle butt. Just as a friendly reminder.

"I hated you damned white coats to begin with," he said. "And you've been playing us for idiots. You have a lot more cards than you're putting on the table. First it was these antimatter-whatever energy orbs. I get that. Fun to weaponize. The Empire brass will be swinging their dicks at half the universe with bombs that can eat entire planets."

Rocky giggled.

"Now it turns out the Union is playing with wormholes?" Lucky said, stabbing a finger at Vlad. "And you have known about it?" He thumbed at the image of the skreamers that were growing larger at an alarming rate. "Right now, we need to get the hell out of this debacle. After that, you're gonna spill your guts, or take a walk outside without a suit."

He turned and locked eyes with Orton. "Same for you, asshole."

"It doesn't matter," retorted Orton.

He held up his data-harvester arm. It must have been transmitting because the coordinates flashed in his mind. "The anomaly is four thousand klicks out. We'll never make it."

"Rocky?"

"This is as fast as this thing goes in standard space."

Just great. And why the hell were they all looking at him again?

"It might have something to do with punching people," observed Rocky.

"Not helpful." He looked around. "Any ideas?" he said, surveying the Marines. "We won't outrun those skreamers, and Rocky is sure that whatever they throw at us is going to be a lot more like what they did to our destroyers."

Jiang asked, "What weapons do we have?"

"What you see is what you get, baby," said Malby, hands up.

Nico stood up. Lucky realized for the first time that he still had his hammerhead on. The rest of the team had shed theirs when they first arrived at the ship. Jesus, he had to be hot in it.

"I can go out there and slow them down."

The kid was stupid, but he was up for a fight.

Lucky was back to liking him.

Malby rolled his eyes. "Yeah, right. You and a pea-shooter."

"And we collectively have less than half our locust drones still available," Dawson said. "And they are mostly in here."

Lucky looked at Vlad, who was still rubbing her head. "Ideas?"

"There are no conventional weapons on the ship," she said.

Again, Orton was looking at her strangely, as clearly surprised at her depth of knowledge as the rest of them.

"Did we bring one of the battle drones on board?" asked Lucky.

Dawson shook his head.

"I think the kid is right," said Jiang.

Malby looked at her like she had just pissed herself. "What good does sending him out there do?"

"Not him," she said, rolling her eyes at Malby. "That." She nodded at the kid. "We can send the hammerhead out. It won't show on their scans like one of our drones will."

That was a fair point. But there was a reason for that. Malby beat him to it.

"Of course not. What threat are they?"

She looked at Lucky with a crooked smile.

"That clever bitch," Rocky said.

Lucky shook his head. "What am I missing?"

"Nico, shed that hammerhead," she said.

Nico stared.

"Now!"

"Ma'am!" the kid blurted, fumbling for the latches that appeared as his AI pushed his internal bots to release locks.

"Malby," she said. "Get your hot box and reprogram that thing. We don't need precision, just need a hit on one of those incoming skreamers." She looked at him. "Can you do that?"

He shrugged. "I can try."

She looked at Lucky. "And now we just need—"

Before she finished, a locust flashed into the room from

a passageway about a quarter klick away at the far end of the cavernous space that Lucky hadn't even identified. Actually, it was two locusts with an energy band between them. They were carrying a—

"No!" said Vlad, forcefully. "We can't afford to lose another one." She looked at Lucky. "We don't know how many we need to cross the fold. We can't keep losing them."

Lucky realized what was happening now.

"I don't know what she has heard, but the ship isn't worried, so I'm not." Rocky said. *"It isn't happy, mind you, but it doesn't seem like the end of the world."*

The locusts dropped the single orb into the body cavity of the hammerhead. At the same instant, the hammerhead came to life.

"Whoa, uh, maybe we should be careful with that," said Malby, stepping back from his handiwork and eying the orb carefully. "Do you guys feel that?"

Now that he said it, Lucky realized his head was buzzing.

"My readings are all over the place," said Malby.

Jiang and Dawson nodded.

"Freaky," said Cheeky, who was holding his hands over his ears, eyes closed. The interference was getting louder and stronger the longer they stood near the orb.

"We need to get that thing outta here," Lucky said. "I don't know how much more of this we can take."

Lucky hadn't looked closely at it before, but now that he could see it, he saw it was semi-transparent. Minuscule wisps of light kept bouncing up and settling back down in a circular pattern. As it settled in the hammerhead, it pulsed and shifted like a water balloon ready to pop.

His head was screaming now.

The locusts that brought the orb grabbed the hammerhead and rocketed off back down the corridor they had come from.

Instantly, the pressure on his head subsided. He realized Rocky had been saying something to him, but he missed it.

"Rocky, did you—"

Malby yelled and dived.

On the ship's eye, the V-shaped skreamers had again formed the bright light at the front of the lead ship.

A blue beam spewed out, slicing the space between the skreamers and the alien ship.

A high-pitched whine came from the stern of the ship, and the projected image flickered.

The floor fell away, and the gravity with it, and Lucky was left somersaulting weightlessly through the air.

[33]
NOTHING

The gravity rushed back in an angry instant.

He fell several meters and felt his spiders pluck frantically in his mind. He heeded their call at the last second and brought his shoulder around to roll as the ground came up rapidly to meet his face.

He bounced sideways, then felt the knot in his stomach as the gravity shifted around him again.

He looked about.

Malby was facedown and bloody. Dawson and Cheeky looked to be dazed.

Jiang was holding her shoulder.

Only Nico and Vlad looked like they had been able to brace themselves in time.

Malby's pulse rifle had slid across the floor in the craziness, and for just a split second Lucky saw Vlad's eyes wander down to it.

She was thinking about it, he thought. Then she glanced up at Lucky and quickly looked away.

The ship's eye flickered back to life.

The kamikaze hammerhead carved lazily through space in big swooping turns.

He was about to bitch to Malby about his technical skills when he realized the Marine was unconscious.

"Get the hot box!" he yelled.

Malby had dropped it.

Jiang picked it up but turned immediately to Lucky. "How the hell does this thing work?"

Hot boxes were a bit of a mystery to anyone unfamiliar with them. Most of the magic was performed at the nanobot level, and the only Marine here with the right gear baked into him was currently knocked out.

On the ship's eye, the skreamers began to come around for another pass.

"We have to wake up Malby," he said. "Maybe if we just—"

He stopped talking. The lead skreamer flew directly into the meandering hammerhead.

"We were due for a break," Rocky noted dryly. *"Guess we used our one up."*

For a moment, Lucky wasn't so sure. He thought it had missed.

And then the familiar pinpoint of light erupted.

The lead skreamer was engulfed in dark red flame. It was something like what they had seen on the surface, but it had a different quality from this close range.

Close range.

"Rocky, get us outta here!"

"Working on it."

"Work harder!"

The ship was listing badly but began to roll sharply away from the skreamers.

As one skreamer after another flamed up and disappeared, the rest lost discipline and started peeling off in different directions. But the flame easily leapt from one to the next, leaving a thin thread between them.

Then Lucky saw another thread appear, extending from the last skreamer to a Union destroyer.

How was that possible? There was nothing there, no matter to leap through, and yet the antimatter clearly found some breadcrumbs to follow.

In a blink, the port side of the destroyer flared and was devoured. He could see for just a split second the exposed floors of the ship with men and women inside, running along corridors. Others ripped out of sleeping quarters. Out the latrines.

They disappeared as fast as the flame crawled over the destroyer.

Then it was gone. Completely gone.

And then the thin line appeared again, and the dance repeated itself with the sister destroyer.

And then it jumped again. And again.

Lucky saw there were remnants of their own armada in higher orbit. The Union destroyers had been picking over the remains. Perhaps looking for survivors. Perhaps killing them.

But they were all flashing and disappearing now. The entirety of ships and wreckage and drones in high orbit. Gone.

And then the thread lazily latched on to the ancient ship.

The flame began to descend upon them.

"Rocky!"

His spiders went into overtime as strings of data arrived with the flame. Even his spiders—who loved a good challenge—were overwhelmed.

Vlad wasn't moving, just staring transfixed at the image on the screen. "It's beautiful," she said.

"Focused energy patterns in stasis. It works just like you said," Orton said. "It's following the patterns, connecting the dots. How did you know?"

"It's looking like it's going to eat us," said Dawson, cool and calm as ever.

He's not wrong, Lucky thought.

"Lucky!" Jiang yelled in his direction.

"Rocky? Thoughts?"

"He is wrong," echoed Rocky. *"We are at the coordinates."*

"What? Where?"

Lucky stared into the view screen projected in the room.

There was nothing there.

They came all this way, did all this for a big fat nothing.

Why had he been so stupid as to believe Vlad? But what could he do? And why would she lie?

And now they were going to die in the middle of nowhere, devoured by some alien hocus-pocus.

He considered shooting Vlad out of spite when something in his mind drew his attention.

The spiders sensed something.

They were pulsing forward, buzzing. He hadn't felt their will this strong before.

Data was pouring in from somewhere.

He looked at the ship's eye. But try as he might, Lucky couldn't see anything.

He put his nose right up to the image. He willed something to appear.

Nothing.

And then he realized that was exactly what he should be looking for.

"No stars," he said.

It was a complete void.

But his spiders sure saw something. Could pattern-recognition bots hyperventilate? If so, that's what they were doing.

A pattern of more and more complex lines formed in his head. This was nothing like a spider web. It was a quilt. It was a fabric. It was more lines of data than he had ever sensed.

A tiny dark spot expanded in front of his face, growing until the pitch-black point had engulfed them.

And then it was simply darkness.

It must be the antimatter eating us, he thought.

This must be what it feels like to become nothing at all.

[34]
HAPPY GIANT

Hello, nightmare.

But this wasn't the nightmare. For once, he wasn't reliving the experiments. The torture. The Hate.

It was just a dream.

He opened his eyes to a room of walls folding in on themselves. Within the walls, threads intertwined, lined up and marching around. Each wall fell back into itself to form a new wall with a new, slightly shifted pattern of threads.

The process kept repeating, with the tiny variations building on each, one after another.

And then he saw his spiders.

He had always pictured them in his mind as spiders, crawling over lines of data. But he knew they were really tiny, nearly invisible pattern-recognition nanobots crawling around and over and through the neurons in his brain.

But now he wasn't just picturing them in his mind. He was actually looking at them. Seeing them. Tiny mechanical spiders.

How is this possible?

And then he realized he wasn't alone.

There was a woman walking along the walls, running her fingers over the spiders. They crawled around and over her fingers as she plucked at the patterns of thread.

She looked up at Lucky and froze.

"How are you here?"

Lucky couldn't speak.

He was looking at his sister. His sister, who had died when he was still in training. His sister, who had been the greatest pilot in the fleet, the sister who deserved better than to die on some routine mission in the middle of nowhere forgotten by everyone while Lucky was known and celebrated and had drinks named after him for doing nothing more than surviving.

She was the one who was great. He was the one who lived.

"Libby?" he said.

The woman blinked.

"It's me, Lucky.

"It's Rocky."

Lucky stared. The voice was wrong. But this was his sister as he remembered her. As she had been when he had last seen her all those decades ago.

The woman wrinkled up her nose.

"You're picturing me as your sister? Gross. What the hell is wrong with you?"

Well, it was Rocky, that much was sure.

Lucky opened his mouth, but nothing came out. He closed it again.

Rocky nodded her head. "Exactly."

She sighed. "You aren't really seeing any of this, of course. This is a construct inside your mind, you big dummy." She paused. "Your sister. What the hell." She shook her head and continued. "Look, I don't know exactly what the ship is doing. But I know that it's using our pattern-recognition bots to do it." She reached out to one of the walls, and the spiders swarmed around her hand. "We are navigating the path the ship is taking."

Lucky frowned. "Navigating through what?"

"The endless universes," said a new voice.

Another woman entered the room. It was Jiang, but again the voice was wrong.

Rocky snorted in derision. "Damn, Lucky, you gotta meet more women." She nodded her head. "Ship, Lucky. Lucky, Ship."

"So this isn't Jiang, and you aren't"—he swallowed —"Libby. So how am I seeing all this?"

"Like I said, you aren't really seeing any of this. It's a mental construct. But why or how you entered it, I'm not sure."

"It's not unusual for this interaction to happen with the navigator during a transit," said the Ship.

"When a what does what now?"

But the Ship wasn't listening. It was looking at Lucky. "You are like the ones inside me."

"That's what she said," Rocky whispered under her breath, all but erasing any doubt as to her identity.

The Ship seemed fascinated. "What is it like?"

"What is what like?"

"To be ..." the Ship paused. "You."

Rocky broke in. "Are we getting close?" she said to the Ship.

The Ship waved her away. "You will know."

Lucky looked at Rocky. "What is she asking me?"

"She has never seen humans before. Or anything except Da'hune."

"Da what?"

At that moment, he felt a ripple in the room. A red, wispy cloud circled in the corner of his eye. If the others noticed, they didn't react.

"Da'hune," said Rocky. "That is what her race is, or the race that built her. The even named her. She said something unintelligible. It translates to *Happy Giant*."

"Happy Giant," Lucky said. "The ancient alien starship we are on right now is called *Happy Giant*?"

"Roughly," said Rocky. "I didn't name it. The Da'hune did."

Back to them. Lucky was sure he should have a million questions right now, but none were coming to mind.

"How old are you, uh, *Happy Giant*?" he asked at last.

"Eight billion of your years," she said, seeming to look at Rocky for confirmation.

Lucky sensed that most of this conversation—if you could call it that—was happening through Rocky. Just as she had first interacted with the Ship when they came on board, Lucky sensed that she was the key to the communication going the other way as well.

"At the time of the purge."

Lucky didn't like the sound of that. "The purge?"

"Yes, to protect the offspring. The others were cleansed from the near-space in order to allow the offspring to grow in a safe environment."

Lucky looked at Rocky. "Does that mean what I think it means?"

Rocky shrugged. "Takes one submission specialist to recognize another."

He shook his head. "They killed off all the other races to keep their offspring pure?"

The Ship grimaced. "All of life is dying. We hastened their change for the sake of the offspring."

All of life is dying. Lucky would have agreed with that statement if it weren't for the whole genocide vibe.

The room rippled again. This time he was sure of it.

"Did you see that?" he asked Rocky.

She cocked her head. "See what?"

Lucky looked again, thought he saw the red wispy cloud again, this time flowing in and out of the data streams with the spiders. "That," he said pointing. But there was nothing there.

The Ship continued, "Before that, we had of course spent billions of years growing our nest." She indicated the walls that the spiders were still diligently dancing upon. "We built millions of corridors that allowed us to step across the distances of our nest."

"Corridors," Lucky said, looking at Rocky.

"Wormholes," she replied. "Or folds if you prefer. They had millions of these, but they are gone now."

Lucky stared at Rocky.

"You get what that means, right?" she said, pointedly.

Lucky nodded soberly.

Rocky shook her head. "Don't get all soft on me. What it means is that this is the reason all the relics we have ever found are all from the same universal time. The Da'hune simply entered their corridors and arrived where they wanted to exterminate next. They could literally be everywhere in the universe at once."

The power of the corridors started to sink in. Everywhere at once.

"Are they still there?" he said. "Still here?"

Rocky said, "This seems to be the only one, and—"

The Ship harrumphed. "This corridor is poorly made. It is deficient. The Da'hune would not have used it in this condition."

Rocky addressed the Ship. "This isn't a Da'hune corridor?"

The room rippled again. Every time they said the word Da'hune, he realized.

The Ship laughed. "Oh no." She froze for a moment, then continued. "Other than the Great Corridor, I can sense no others in the nest."

Rocky said, "The Great Corridor?"

"The nest is the known universe," Rocky said matter-of-factly to Lucky. She turned to the Ship. "What is the Great Corridor?"

"Have we not spoken of it?"

"No."

"It is a wonder. All the great Da'hune together built it. This universe is imprisoned within a black hole, which itself is imprisoned in a black hole at the universal center of the first birthplace. The Great Corridor resides on the overlap of two twinned universes."

Lucky looked at Rocky. She just shrugged. "That explains it."

"They found a new place with it," continued the Ship. "A new place to start over and fix the mistakes that had come before," she said. "It was a mistake to destroy the cultures, or so the great council said. The ecosystem needs the diversity, even if it is puny and weak. It was for the health of the offspring."

The Ship seemed to draw itself up a little taller. "I was among the great wave. Born to take the Da'hune through the Great Corridor."

It was a nice speech that made almost no sense to Lucky. But Rocky was looking thoughtful.

"And why are you here?"

The Ship looked bitter. "The Da'hune fell upon themselves. The council was not fully supported. I was left behind."

Lucky waited for an elaboration, but it was clear there was nothing more to come.

"And so we came to find you here," he said. "And now you are purging us, as well."

The Ship roared with laughter. "You were not here when the purge occurred. Your survival ... It is no small thing, certainly, but ..." the Ship shrugged. "I am not Da'hune. I have not been for billions of years. There are no offspring here to purge for."

"But then, what is happening out there?"

The Ship looked at Rocky. "You asked the same, did you not?"

Rocky said to Lucky, "She doesn't seem to know anything about what is happening out there."

"How is that possible? This is what all this is about, is it not?" He thought about all the eyeless freaks attacking them. About the attack on their fleet. "Unless—"

This time the ripple was unmistakable, as was the red mist. He felt his eyes begin to water. He quickly bent over to get below the cloud, but there was nowhere to go. It was filling his lungs with burning and rage.

"Blasphemy!" he screamed in rage. But it wasn't his voice. It was wild and jealous and furious. "To purge is to live!"

The Hate descended on him in total control. He flew violently through the air. He felt something crunch in his hands, felt something gurgle and pop. His face was wet and twisted. He opened his eyes.

Jiang's head was crushed, barely recognizable under his bloody hands.

And then he was laughing—a deep, mirthful, evil laugh.

The spiders abruptly stopped dancing.

The Hate was happy.

Lucky was crying. He wanted to kill himself.

[35]
ARRIVING

Lucky reached up for his face. It was wet, but when he pulled back, his hands weren't red. They weren't covered in blood. Only in his tears.

Through his blurry eyes, he realized The Hate had left him.

He looked around. The others were splayed about on the floor.

"Oh no ... what did I do?" he whispered.

"Relax, Lucky. You didn't do anything. It was a bumpy ride."

Malby crawled on his hands and knees. "What the hell was that?"

He looked groggy, and Lucky remembered he had been knocked out earlier.

But now it looked like they all had.

Jiang was sitting up now as well. "Antimatter?"

Orton shook his head. "We wouldn't be here," he said.

Nico was dazed, his eyelids fluttering, and Lucky wondered why he couldn't seem to interact with his AI without telegraphing it.

Orton was holding Vlad by the shoulder, still staring daggers at Lucky.

"What the hell is that?" said Dawson, pointing at the ship's eye.

Lucky tried to make sense of what he was seeing. The perspective was wrong.

"Did the view change?" he asked aloud but directed to Rocky.

"Negative," she replied.

"How is that possible?" he said, still aloud.

"Better find something to hang on to."

The others were looking at him questioningly, only hearing one side of the conversation.

Looming up in the ship's eye was a massive wall draped with the same ore the ancient ship was made from. The same ore that had, as Lucky recalled, survived close-range nuke blasts and destroyer cannons.

"Brace yourself!" Lucky yelled as he took a knee.

Jiang and Dawson reacted immediately, hitting the deck. Nico joined them a moment later.

The two scientists were already leaning next to one of the huge alien-scripted sheer walls that segmented the space.

Malby swung his head around to stare at the ship's eye. In typical Malby fashion, he took no action to brace himself. "Why—"

The floor jerked hard out from below them. Even from his place on the ground, Lucky was flung forward.

Malby, already off balance, flew off his feet and directly into Lucky.

Lucky tried to turn to take some of the hit to his shoulder, but in the process he caught Malby under the chin.

The big Marine flipped over, legs flailing in the air before landing upside down on his back.

"What part of brace yourself wasn't clear?" Lucky said.

Malby didn't respond. He didn't move. Lucky realized that his shoulder to the chin had knocked Malby out again.

"Nicely done," Rocky said. *"It almost seemed like an accident."*

Lucky looked back at the ship's eye and instinctively raised his pulse rifle, which he didn't even remember reaching for.

He was staring at a woman in black Union gear. He knew she wasn't right there. He knew the ship's eye was showing them the outside of the ship. But it *felt* like she was right there.

It wasn't clear which of them was more surprised. The soldier staring at the business end of an alien ship—or Lucky staring into what he expected to be space and instead finding the bewildered eyes of a Union soldier.

Lucky guessed it was her.

Three more soldiers scuttled past the woman as they struggled with something in front of her. Lucky realized he was looking at a control room mounted above the sheer ore wall they had just slammed into.

The alien ship was floating free now, sliding lazily backward from the impact.

Lucky couldn't seem to get his bearings. He wasn't the only one.

"What is this?" said Jiang. "What's going on?"

"We were just. In the middle. Of space," Dawson said emphatically.

"This can't be what is really out there," said Cheeky, shaking his head. "Could this be, I don't know, a view from somewhere inside the ship or somewhere else or…" he trailed off.

"You don't just go from space to a,"—Jiang searched for the right word; she pointed to the control room—"a space station hangar."

Lucky stared ahead, stunned. He saw it now. She was right. It was a space station hangar.

Even Jiang seemed a little surprised at her leap, but now that she said it, they all saw it.

This was a situation he had been in hundreds of times in his life. Thousands. He was sitting in a ship in a shipyard, looking up at the control tower.

There was one big difference, of course. In all of his previous experience, he hadn't been flying along in deep space a moment before instantaneously appearing in space dock.

"Minor details," said Rocky. She didn't seem the least bit rattled.

"Rocky, can we get drones out there?" he echoed.

"Already on it."

His mind's eye was instantly filled with a rapidly expanding view as the drone he was looking through zoomed away from the ship.

Lucky saw hundreds of Union destroyers, all draped in the same gray ore as *Happy Giant*.

They all looked like copies of each other, right down to the bulbous stern section that looked out of place with what he knew of standard Union tech.

These weren't just more alien-infused pieces of Union tech. They were far more alien than Union. The ships were docked edge to edge as if they were sitting in storage.

As the view continued expanding, Lucky began to

understand why he wasn't seeing stars. This was an enclosed space.

An enormous enclosed space. Easily the largest hangar he had ever seen in his life.

"That's saying a lot from an old man like you," said Rocky.

The Empire had the largest space docks in the known universe—and with the exception of a couple of private hubs in the Cardinal Order, the largest man-made facilities in existence.

This dwarfed them all. He could stuff all the stations he had ever visited in here, and there would still be room left over to stuff it full of, well, of these Union-alien hybrid ships.

The drone had stopped pulling away, but he still couldn't see an end of the Union destroyers. They were leaking out of his mind's eye on both sides.

"Rocky, this seems like bad news for our team."

Lucky focused closer on *Happy Giant* and the sheer ore wall they had rushed headlong into.

It was attached to the wall of the hangar itself, and that gray-banded ore extended all around the entire sphere of the hangar.

And it was a sphere. There was scaffolding attached at various points, and Lucky saw how it supported the ore excavation points. This is where the ore was coming from. They had literally hollowed out the inside of the asteroid as they built these ships.

"This is the X point," said Orton, who was standing right behind him.

For a second, Lucky wondered how Orton was seeing through his mind's eye.

Then he realized he was pointing at the image in the

ship's eye, which was still transferring an image from directly in front of the ship.

"This is the hollowed-out space that our spy described," he said excitedly, turning to Vlad.

Lucky looked between them. "You recognize this place?"

Vlad nodded cautiously. "Perhaps. It does fit the description."

"Of what?"

"Of their hidden testing location. The reason we couldn't see what they were up to," she said. "This is their skunkworks, where they do all their alien outfitting."

But now it was Orton shaking his head. "But this can't be it."

"You just said it was," Dawson said.

"But if that really is where we are, then we would have to be—"

"Inside the Union home system," Vlad finished.

Lucky whipped around.

"The Union system? That's more than three-hundred light years from the outer fringe," said Jiang dismissively.

"Exactly right."

Lucky echoed to Rocky, *"Holy hell, the Ship wasn't lying."*

"You thought it was?"

"I—Yeah, I guess I did. Or at least exaggerating."

"Well, I have more interesting news for you courtesy of our friend the Ship."

"Do tell."

"It comes in two flavors. Bad news and worse news."

"Color me shocked. What's the bad news?"

"Those destroyers with the fat asses? They all have T'ket'ka in them. Each one of them."

"You mean each one of these destroyers has one of those antimatter orbs in them, the same ones that we just watched eat a small planet?"

"The very same."

"That's just the bad news? What's the worse news?"

"We're about to get boarded."

[36]
LEAD ON

"CAN you tell the Ship to take us back through the fold?"

"You don't think I already thought about that? They've anchored us already."

Lucky should have thought about that.

This was a port, after all, so having anchoring beams would be a must. The ion beams would hold the ship in place easily from this close distance.

"Besides, I can't reach the Ship anymore."

"What?"

"You heard me. It went dark when the anchoring beams hit. I don't know if that's a coincidence or what."

"No," echoed Lucky. *"They have a huge head start on us with this tech. I'm sure they know exactly how to use it. We have no cards here."*

Rocky switched his mind's eye view to another locust drone, this one just off the starboard bow, so he could get a better sense of the situation right next to the alien ship.

The ship had come to rest on a large assembly that jutted out from the ore edge of the hollowed-out asteroid.

The long flat platform was more than twice as long as

the alien ship and at least five times as wide. Lucky couldn't see below, but he imaged it was solid ore, a landing platform of sorts left untouched in the excavation work.

At the far end of the platform was a colossal arch, more than twice as wide again as the alien ship. On the outside of the gate was more alien script. Lucky was struck by how much it reminded him of the access points within *Happy Giant*. And again, he realized it was the script itself telling him that. But as he looked at the arch, he realized what he wasn't seeing.

He didn't see what was on the other side. He only saw a flat wall of pitch-black nothingness. Just what he had seen before they transited the Great Corridor, as the Ship had called it.

This was the terminus of the corridor they had just passed through.

On the platform directly in front of the arches, equipment was strewn everywhere.

Scientists in white coats—always white coats!—were running around like a supernova just exploded in their collective minds, their shocked faces looking at the alien ship, pointing and yelling.

Along with artificial gravity, there must have been breathable atmosphere being pumped in.

"I think we now know why the Ship was so unimpressed with the corridor," Rocky echoed. *"It was clearly built by Union scientists using Da'hune technology."*

Lucky took a moment to consider this. The magnitude of what the Union had accomplished here was stunning. Even with access to the amazing technology he had seen in action, this was breathtaking.

He looked again at all the scientist scurrying around the platform before coming back to his senses.

Where there are eggheads in white coats, there are sure to be—

"Here come those soldiers," said Rocky.

Lucky saw them too, now, Union soldiers pouring onto the platform from walkways that led across the connection with the ore side of the hangar.

"Lock and load, Marines," said Jiang, beating Lucky to the punch. "We got company."

He realized the Marines had been watching the stream of soldiers flow onto the platform from the ship's eye.

They wore standard black Union combat gear, and Lucky had no doubt they were kitted out with the same alien technology that the Marines were already all too familiar with.

Jiang, Dawson, and Nico had their pulse rifles out. They were deploying their drones as well, what few they had left.

"On the plus side, they have eyes," Rocky offered.

Lucky looked at Orton and Vlad. "Any ideas from the cheap seats?"

Vlad tore her eyes away from the display. "Yes, actually. We got a good look at the layout when we were in the stack-shack reading the first team's progress. There's a small interior hangar farther forward."

Orton was shaking his head, but Vlad ignored him.

"We're being boarded from the bow," Lucky said, nodding at the divisions of soldiers pouring onto the platform. "I'm not terribly keen on running into them."

Vlad was adamant. "We can escape that way."

"Explain," Lucky said.

"There are more alien vessels there. Smaller, more maneuverable. I'm sure your ... Rocky, will be able to communicate with them just as she has this ship."

"Wait," said Jiang to Lucky. "Why can't you just have your AI turn us around right now and get out of here?"

Lucky quickly brought them up to speed on the anchoring beam and the sudden silence of the Ship.

"So, we are on our own, now?" asked Jiang.

"Seems so."

Dawson took his turn to speak up. "Even if we do manage to get back across that fold thing, can't they just follow us?"

Vlad shook her head.

"Don't you see this?" she said, nodding at the ship's eye view. She waved her arms at the scientists scrambling around the platform, gathering equipment that had scattered and blown everywhere. "They didn't expect anything to come through that fold. I don't believe they knew something could."

"That's quite an assumption," said Jiang.

"Consider how we found it. We triangulated a signal that was using the downloaded Trojan package to control the miners on that planet."

"So?"

"So, why would they have all this set up here to send that signal if they were actively using the fold for transport?"

"What are you saying?"

Orton spoke up now. "They controlled them using quantum entanglements," he said. "That much we could ascertain from the signal."

"Say again?"

"It activated entangled particles on the other side of the fold. By collapsing the superpositions, they instantaneously changed their—"

Lucky held up his hand. "I don't need a science lesson. What is your point?"

"The point is that they need incredible amounts of energy and a huge investment to do it," said Vlad.

"If they could just go through the fold rather than transmit across it, don't you think they would have?"

Nico spoke up. "Didn't they do that already, though? Remember how those destroyers came out of nowhere to attack our armada."

Vlad gave Nico a withering stare, and the kid shut up.

"They were there the whole time. We knew they were there. Why do you think we brought superior firepower?" She looked back at Lucky. "Or at least what we thought was superior."

Lucky cocked an eyebrow but didn't disagree. They had underestimated this whole operation from top to bottom. No way to argue that point.

"The sabotage," Rocky echoed.

"Come again?"

"Even with the alien tech, I don't know if the Union force we saw could overwhelm our armada. The Empire expected trouble."

Lucky was following now.

"But someone managed to send the armada to kingdom come before the Union forces even arrived."

If Lucky was being honest, he'd forgotten about the sabotage. It seemed impossible to believe, but they had bigger issues to deal with. "Okay, so they can't go through the fold, but we can? They have all this alien tech here. How could they not just do what we just did?"

"Because they have alien tech that they have fused with their own tech. But we didn't use our tech at all, did we? We used their ancient ship to go through their ancient fold."

Lucky didn't mention what the Ship had said about the fold. This wasn't a Da'hune fold. This was made by Union scientists using Da'hune technology as a template.

But that seemed to support what Vlad was saying. They didn't know what they had.

"So," Lucky said, "we need to get to this other hangar stocked with smaller alien ships that haven't been hit with their docking beam. Then we dive back through the fold before they have a chance to stop us, and we get the hell out of this nightmare and find someone else to give this problem to."

Vlad nodded.

Lucky looked around at the Marines.

"Easy peasy."

He reached down and with one arm yanked Malby into the air and slammed him over his shoulder. He felt a stimulant cocktail run through his bloodstream, upping his chemical levels. The boost of strength wasn't much, but it made Malby feel that much lighter.

He pointed his rifle in Vlad's face.

"Lead on."

[37]
LITTLE GIANTS

JIANG WAS on point with Cheeky on her ass, a place he clearly wanted to be.

Nico and Dawson were in back, watching everyone else's asses.

He felt Malby shift his weight.

"Why the hell am I looking at your ass?" Malby asked.

Lucky jerked up his shoulder and shoved the big lug off backward, sending him flipping over his back.

Malby landed in a sprawling heap.

"Ouch!"

Lucky stretched his arms over his sore shoulders. "Glad you're awake. Try and actually brace yourself next time a superior tells you to brace yourself."

"Where the fuck are we?"

Lucky had no interest in bringing the big idiot up to speed. "We're going on a little field trip. There will be men with guns. You should get yours out."

"What are you—"

"What did I just say about listening to rank?"

Malby grumbled but pulled his rifle out. "Since when did you decide to act like an officer?"

Lucky flinched. That hurt.

"You are getting a little officer-ish," noted Rocky. *"And since you're acting like you care now, you should know; they just splashed my two exterior locusts."*

That sobered Lucky up. "They are coming in," he said. "Where are we on the drone spread?"

Malby had been out cold thirty seconds ago, but he was up to speed now. God bless their AI. "We have a partial defensive spread, but only a half-klick nose to ass."

"That's it?"

"That's it. Or maybe you weren't around for us getting our ass kicked once already today? We are at 20 percent spread."

Jiang said, "Can we go offensive with that?"

Malby shrugged.

"We should have brought one of those stingrays with us," said Dawson.

"Didn't the other Marines bring battle platforms?" asked Cheeky over his shoulder.

"Your comrades did not enter the ship," said Vlad. "They set up at the ship's base."

"Contacts!" yelled Malby.

"Where?" Lucky yelled, as the Marines tensed.

"Straight ahead," he said, eyes glazed over as the tech specialist worked with his AI.

"How many?"

"A whole hell of a lot, a little less than a klick out," he said. Then he shrugged. "I'd say five minutes if we go straight at 'em."

"Tighten up, and double-time it," demanded Lucky.

"Malby, draw 'em in for max cover. Keep eyes forward, though."

The group moved off at a trot.

Lucky fell back next to Nico. "Remember what I said earlier about not being a hero?"

Nico nodded.

"Good. Don't be a hero."

Jiang said, "Lucky, I get your life credo and all. But some of us are here because we want to be."

"Yeah, we all wanted to be here once," Malby said.

Jiang shook her head. "Malby, you're conscripted. Don't tell me you want to be here."

"Beats prison," he said. Then he thought about what he was saying. "Or it used to." He shook his head. "Anyway, don't give me crap. You're a conscript, too, right?"

She shook her head again. "No, my brother was, the little jackass thief. I followed him in. To keep an eye on him."

Malby nodded in understanding. "When my sister got into an all-girls school, I tried to follow her in, too."

Nico chuckled.

Jiang didn't seem to hear.

"How long, Malby?" Lucky huffed, finally starting to feel the effects of the trot.

"Four minutes."

Jiang didn't look winded at all. Again, she was absently rubbing the chain around her neck.

He'd seen that fossilized fang that hung from it before. He knew it.

"Rocky?" Damn it, he wished he didn't get his freezer burned so much.

Then something clicked in the useless caverns of his shitty memory.

Yes, he did recognize it! The tooth was from a tannierian devil. He used to have one just like. They were rare. Really rare.

He thought back to her words from earlier. 'My brother worships the ground you walk on.'

I knew her brother, he realized. *I gave that to her brother*.

This close connection to Jiang hit him like a pulse to the gut.

"I'm thinking," said Dawson. He was staring straight ahead, pumping his legs.

Lucky hadn't even realized he was listening. He was still coming to terms with his revelation about Jiang's brother. He suddenly felt like he needed urgently to talk to her about it, but Dawson plunged ahead.

"Running hasn't helped me. It hasn't helped my little girl."

He didn't seem like the running type to Lucky.

He turned with that lanky smile. "I'll just hang close to our lucky charm here."

"I'm a lot of things," Lucky said. "But I'm no lucky charm."

"That's not what I hear," said Vlad. The scientist was easily keeping pace.

Orton was huffing along beside her despite having no gear to carry.

"Oh so lucky," said Rocky.

"Three minutes," shouted Malby.

Lucky yelled at Vlad, "How close are these ships of yours?"

As he said it, the corridor broadened.

"We're here."

The group stopped to survey the space. It looked almost identical to the one they had been in. Smaller was a relative term. It was still more than a half-klick wide and just as tall. It had fewer pathways leading into it, which was a plus. One wall harbored the same alien script and set of matching arches. The access points. Unlike the earlier ones, the bands here were shifted in a different formation from the rest of the ore wall. They were detached and separate.

But the real tactical advantage was what was inside. It was full of big, featureless blocks of rock. The blocks were thrown around and jumbled, many on their sides.

Lucky spotted one that was flipped over. The underside had an array of pins that connected to a central disk.

It dawned on Lucky that these were the ships Vlad was talking about. And in that context, and knowing the composition of *Happy Giant*, it made sense. They shared the same exterior of overlocking sheets of banded gray ore. Arched openings were set into the side of each one.

But they were still massive. The entire party could fit into one with plenty of space to spare.

"Those are your idea of small, maneuverable ships?" yelled Malby as the group ran across the open hangar.

"No!" yelled Vlad, breathing easily. "But they were to the builders of this ship. And they were only interested in fold passage."

It made sense. *Happy Giant* was a single-purpose vehicle, and so were these. Everything here was entirely devoted to transit with the Da'hune through the Great Corridor.

No wonder the Ship was pissy about getting left behind.

"Also," she said, "small is relative. We believe the aliens were at least three times our size."

That tracked with the oversized nature of *Happy Giant*. It was also a very sobering thought in light of the conversation with the Ship in transit.

"Two minutes!" yelled Malby.

"Move!" bellowed Lucky.

If this all went to hell, they needed to settle into cover. And he already knew it was going to go to hell.

"You picking anything up, Rocky?"

"Negative."

That's what Lucky had been afraid of.

This plan was doomed.

[38]

LEAVING

"How are our readings, Malby?"

Malby looked curiously at Lucky. "Come again?"

"You getting any interference?"

Malby shook his head. "No, why?"

They reached the nearest of the small ships, which Lucky decided to call Little Giant. He leaned against the access point on the side and it slid open with ease.

"Defensive positions!"

Jiang looked over sharply. "Why? Just get Rocky to fly us the hell out of here!"

But Lucky was looking at Vlad now. "But we can't, can we?" he said.

Her eyes widened. "I didn't know."

"Bullshit."

Lucky flipped the clip on his pulse rifle in one practiced action, spinning the weapon on his palm.

Then he shot her.

Vlad exhaled sharply as she was thrown off her feet, the blast folding her head down to meet her feet, which in turn quickly rose above her head, and she somersaulted backward, flipping over and landing facedown.

"What the hell, Lucky!" screamed Jiang.

Lucky frowned at Jiang. "It was just a stunner."

"Wicked," said Cheeky with a grin.

"Vlad!" screamed Orton as he ran to her side.

"But why?" said Jiang.

Lucky looked over at Malby. "Time?"

Malby seemed to shake himself out of a stupor.

"Uh, one minute, give or take."

The Marines instinctively started scanning.

"Rocky?"

"I'm working on it," she said. *"This place is crawling with Union dirtbags, especially aft."*

"Work faster."

Lucky turned back to Vlad. Blood spilled from a gash on her head, and she clutched her arm where more blood was seeping out.

"You're going to need to talk fast," he said. "But I'm going to start. You know we can't pass through the fold without those little magical orbs, those T'ket'ka. And there isn't a single one of them here. We'd be getting interference like crazy being this close to them," he said. "Everything you have done since the moment we arrived was about getting those antimatter orbs. You have known everything about them before we got here."

"I didn't—"

"Maybe you didn't notice, but the lies are piling up," he said. "You also said the Marines didn't come inside the ship. But you knew where these little suckers were based on readings you got from your scientist pals inside the ship. Now I'm no CO, but there's no goddamned way that your brainiacs were climbing around this ship, unattended, while the Marines held a circle jerk out front."

Vlad opened her mouth, then closed it.

"You know this, right?" Lucky said to Orton. "I saw your face. She shouldn't know what she knows about the layout, right? She has consistently known way more than you and your research buddies."

Orton glared at Lucky, but he wasn't disagreeing.

"Time!" he barked at Malby.

"Thirty seconds!"

"So, now we're screwed," he said. "Do you have some plan to save your own skin and get these orbs back to your precious Empire handlers? Now would be the time to unveil it to dramatic effect."

Vlad curled her lip. "I don't have to answer to an overgrown monkey with dead sister issues."

Lucky jerked his head back like he'd been punched.

"I know the book on you, Lucky. It's pretty thin. And for the record, everyone I've talked to at command agrees. It would've been better if she'd lived and you'd bought it. But you can't pick who lives and dies. That's war."

"Score one for the bitch," said Rocky. *"Better play your cards."*

Lucky was rattled, but Rocky was right.

"Sounds like something the Da'hune would say," he said.

"That doesn't actually make sense," Rocky offered.

"Shut up."

He just wanted to get the word out there and see how she reacted.

It was Vlad's turn to look like she had been punched.

Orton shook his head. "Who?" he said.

"Ask mama bear," he said.

Orton turned to Vlad, reading her expression. "What is he talking about?"

Lucky answered for her. "This ship was real talkative inside the fold. I've got some answers that I bet your fearless leader here would really love to hear."

"Ask and ye shall receive," interrupted Rocky.

Two energy-banded locust drones burst into the room.

Cheeky jerked his rifle up to his shoulder.

Before he could squeeze off a shot, Lucky kicked the back of his leg, causing him to wobble and fire straight upward.

"Dammit!"

"Trust me, you don't want to be shooting that."

The locusts slipped into the little giant. A pearl-colored orb was suspended between them.

Vlad looked horrified. "You brought one of those here?"

"Well, since you couldn't be bothered," Lucky said. The drones slid the T'ket'ka into the shielded compartment that all the lines along the bottom of the container flowed into.

"We're leaving, Marines!" he yelled. A smile crept onto his face. As soon as they were back through the corridor, this whole thing would be some else's problem. They could figure out what the crazy scientists were up to—Empire and Union.

And he could go back to being very, very drunk and try to forget this whole episode even happened.

And most importantly, never give another order again.

"Hot damn!" said Malby, jumping inside.

Cheeky turned back to the ship doorway.

Jiang began slowly stepping back along the outside lip of the ship.

Farther down the hull of the craft, Dawson and Nico were doing the same.

Finally, Vlad seemed to break. "You're right," she said at last. "I have been hiding information from you. All of you. I didn't know if you could be trusted."

Lucky realized he was holding his breath.

"But you've got it all wrong," she said.

And then the walls caved in on them.

[39]
LIAR

A HUGE EXPLOSION threw them off their feet. The container ship bounced into the air with the blast, and Lucky found the roof and the floor equally unpleasant to bounce against.

Rocky instantly hit him with stims as he felt damage bloom all over his body.

The roof of the container ship was depressed downward, the space they were in now deformed and squeezed like a ground pounder's beer can.

Gray rock ore and debris covered the floor of the hangar and poured into the opening on the side of Little Giant, where Jiang and Cheeky had just been standing.

The shielded home for the orb was intact. He knew it would react to pulse fire. He wasn't sure about getting smashed by falling debris, but it was probably best not to find out.

Jiang was gone.

Cheeky was on the ground, smiling up at Lucky like he'd just been on a roller coaster and couldn't believe how much fun it was. Blood poured from his mouth, nose, and eye. His faceplate was shattered.

Lucky could only see his head, neck and shoulders. The rest of him was pinned under the debris blocking the opening.

But he was wrong. He wasn't pinned. The rest of him was gone, sheared off by the force of the falling debris.

Head, neck and shoulders were all that was left.

"Hey, Lucky, my AI's having some problems here," said Cheeky, startling him.

Lucky leaned down and rested his hand on his shoulder. "Those stims are coming now, buddy. Just rest up; your AI will get you fixed up in no time."

"You're a shitty liar," he said, still smiling.

And then he closed his eyes.

There were a lot of injuries that a Frontier Marine could survive with the help of his biobots, but having your body sheared clean in half wasn't one of them.

Lucky said the only thing he could think of, the thing his father had told him when he was very young and his mother died.

"To live is to die," he said quietly.

It was a shitty expression, but his old man wasn't much for expressions and neither was he. Plus, life was shitty.

He looked around the rest of the crushed cabin of the ship.

Chunks of the interior hung down where the pressure had buckled the supports.

The two scientists were on the ground. Orton had a badly broken leg, almost completely folded back under him. He was twisted at an odd angle, and Lucky worried whether he had internal injuries.

Vlad was in better shape. She still had the bloody wounds from when he'd hit her with the stunner, but now she also had a huge bloody hole in her thigh where she'd been partially impaled against a slab of ore on one edge of the ship.

She stared at Lucky, but her eyelids were fluttering and she had a glazed look on her face. She was in shock, he assumed, but she was conscious.

"Get down and stay down!" he screamed.

Malby was a little dazed beside him but on his feet.

"What the hell happened out there, Malby? I thought the drones were tracking them."

"They were," he said, shaking his head.

"They played us. They knew the layout of the ship, and they knew where we were," Rocky said. *"They blew an entire section of the starboard hangar wall over on us."*

Lucky realized now where all the debris came from. It was the fractured remains of the huge overlocking sheets of gray ore.

"What does it look like now?"

"Strange."

"Show me."

Rocky overlaid a drone view. *"They have the high ground above the rubble,"* she explained. *"But they aren't coming down. They're just sitting up there."*

It was eerily silent in the hangar.

The Union soldiers were sitting patiently, and Lucky was sure his Marines weren't dumb enough to present themselves as targets.

But what were they waiting for? They had superior forces. Just swoop down and end this thing.

"Where is everyone?"

As he said it, Jiang's voice whispered over the all-comm.

"Dawson, I see you. Are you okay?"

"Affirmative, coming to your location now."

Lucky heard several energy blasts.

"Damn. Never mind, I'm pinned."

"Everyone, stay down until we get a plan," Lucky said over all-comm. "Sound off. Where are we?"

"Jiang here. I'm under one of the ships at your nine o'clock, Lucky. Two down from your position."

"Dawson, check. I'm about fifteen-feet from Jiang on her three o'clock. I'm behind one big-ass piece of rock."

"Lucky and Malby here in the ship with the brainiacs," he added. He paused. "Cheeky is down."

No response.

Another pause. "Nico?"

Still nothing.

"Rocky, did we lose the kid?"

"I have his AI. He's out there."

Where? Hiding? Then he saw him.

He must have been blown clear when the wall fell. He was halfway across the hangar, lying motionless amongst the rocks.

"You sure he's alive?"

"RTC in progress. ETA on consciousness is about two minutes."

He'd be dead before that. The Union soldiers may have been holding back, but they wouldn't have a hard time hitting a Marine lying sprawled out making a fine target of himself.

"Uh oh," said Rocky.

"What now?"

"I think I see now what they're waiting for."

His mind's eye showed what her drone was seeing.

A large Union battle platform slid into view, followed by another. And then dozens of Union locusts began buzzing into the hangar.

They were going to smoke them out.

[40]
TANGO

"DRONES INCOMING, FIND COVER!" he yelled over all-comm. *And to Rocky, he barked, "Where the hell are our drones?"*

"Already on it," she said. *"Two can play this hide and seek game."*

On cue, dozens of the Marines' drones poured out of a handful of little giants scattered across the hangar. They had waited to vector in behind the cloud of Union drones.

The element of surprise wasn't going to last long, but in a drone war, seconds could make all the difference.

"We have to get out there," he said to Malby.

They began digging at the rocks trapping them inside the ship. Lucky moved a chunk, and light and sound poured in. And then a blue energy beam shattered the rock where his hand had been.

"Goddammit!" he yelled, lurching back from the hole. Two more energy arcs slapped across the rock in rapid succession, and the pile exploded inward, throwing Lucky and Malby backward.

Two drones charged in.

Lucky leapt forward at the lead drone, cutting off its room to maneuver inside the small space. Its burner was right at eye level. He could see the red heat from the port. He slapped it with his left arm as it fired, the energy beam whizzing wildly over his shoulder, singing the side of his head.

He raised his pulse rifle and fired at point-blank range on the second drone, incinerating it.

He jumped back just as the first drone completed its wild spin in the air and bore back down on him. His spiders plucked at his mind, and he jerked hard to his right, again feeling the blue energy as it streamed past his face.

And then it exploded, chunks ricocheting off Lucky's faceplate.

Malby lowered his pulse rifle.

"Thanks," said Lucky.

"Don't mention it." Malby hustled quickly to the hangar opening. "Now what?"

"We need another distraction, Rocky."

"Okay, but this is all we have."

Another wave of drones poured out of their hiding places, though noticeably thinner in coverage this time.

Luckily for the locusts, the Union drones' battle tactics were piss poor as ever, even with the alien weapons tech. They charged at the defensively positioned locusts and were cut down accordingly.

"Tango up!" Lucky yelled over all-comm.

A moment later he heard the raucous exchange of energy beams and pulse fire.

"Covering!" Jiang said.

"I'm in!" Dawson replied a second later.

"Two at your nine o'clock," Jiang said.

"Covering fire!" yelled Lucky as he rolled out from behind the ore rock he was hiding against.

A blast of heat washed over the top of his head, and for the third time in as many minutes he sensed an energy beam slice over his head.

He crawled fast, using the large gray slabs of the collapsed wall as cover.

Nico was right where Rocky's drones had triangulated him. Lucky grabbed him by the leg and turned around.

His spiders plucked hard at his side, and he swung his rifle arm up wildly, firing off a pulse toward the ragged fringe of the collapsed wall.

The kid was heavy as hell to drag in all his combat armor. Then suddenly he wasn't, and Lucky toppled forward over a boulder as yet another blue beam blasted past.

He felt a dull pain in his side.

He glanced back to see he was holding the kid's combat boot, sliced cleanly off at the shin.

He threw it down.

"*Same one,*" Rocky noted wryly.

"*Not now!*"

He rolled back and grabbed the kid's other leg and started dragging again.

A Union drone dropped out of nowhere, but one of the locusts kamikazied into it, and both spun away into the debris field.

Lucky launched Nico into the crushed little ship like a live grenade, then lunged in after him.

Lucky spotted blood spewing from his own flank.

Malby had stationed himself at the opening of the ship, firing away without hitting much of anything.

"We have zero tactical advantage here!" he screamed over the sound of his own pulse rifle.

"You don't say."

With the air temporarily cleared of drones, they'd become easier targets for those Union sharpshooters firing down from the jagged edge of the partially collapsed hanger wall.

Then Lucky felt his spiders go berserk and he looked up to see the battle platforms start moving.

In front of them, three-dozen Union troopers in full battle gear were navigating a descent down the pile of debris.

"Malby—"

But the rock Malby was leaning against exploded, and he fell back awkwardly.

The troops advanced openly now, free of Malby's pulses and shielded from Jiang and Dawson's fire.

Lucky was about to ask Rocky if she had any more drones hiding out in the other ships when he looked down.

The shielded container was intact, he noted.

So was the orb.

"Jiang," Lucky said into the all-comm. "I have a really bad idea."

"I like it already," she replied through the sound of pulse fire.

"Be over in a sec."

"Wait, what?"

[41]
TWO-STEP

"I TAKE IT BACK," she said over the all-comm.

"Too late," Lucky said.

He'd emerged slowly from the rubble of the fallen wall, clutching the T'ket'ka orb in his right hand above his head.

In his left hand he held his pulse rifle with the barrel shoved into the soft bottom of the orb, compressing a deep dimple into it.

A warm wash of electricity spilled down his hand as if someone had left an energy spout open. His head buzzed.

He stopped at the summit of the pile, squeezed his eyes shut, and waited to get shot.

Malby hid just behind the debris-strewn lip of the ship, perched ready to grab Lucky and haul him back if the Union soldiers called his bluff.

Lucky wouldn't bet five credits on himself lasting another five seconds.

One.

Here it comes.

Two.

He clenched his teeth.

Three.

Any second.

Four.

Or maybe—

Five.

He opened one eye.

Then the other.

He felt his ass unclench the tiniest amount.

Then he shoved harder into the side of the orb and started easing the trigger on his rifle.

Even if the Union understood what he had there—and their retrofitting of their destroyers seemed to indicate they did—there was no guarantee these monkeys with guns would know better than to just shoot him. If he were in their shoes he would shoot first and ask forgiveness later.

Luckily for Lucky, his counterpart wasn't out there.

There was a shuffling somewhere along the Union line. What might have been a yell. Then several of the large energy beam rifles wavered and disappeared.

The battle troopers came to a stop.

"Ummm. I didn't really plan for success."

"Have you ever?"

"Fair point."

He inched slowly back toward Malby, careful to keep the orb between himself and the wall of Union soldiers.

"You're up, sport."

Malby stayed crouched in his spot behind the debris. "No way, man."

"Way."

"What about them?" he said, hooking his thumb back at the scientists in the smashed ship.

"Nico can hang back with them while his foot regens," he said. "Orton will have to be carried, anyway, and I don't trust Vlad."

He didn't voice his other thought, which was that if this went south, it was all academic anyway.

"In the meantime, you'll be tactically useful over there."

He slowly rotated back around and backed his ass into Malby's personal space. "So come kiss my ass."

Malby cursed under his breath.

"Nuts to butt, Marine. That's an order."

Malby stood quickly and grabbed Lucky in a bear hug from behind. He bumped up against Lucky's arms, and for one terrifying moment Lucky thought he would drop the orb.

"Goddammit, Malby," he hissed. "Do you not understand the concept of no sudden movements?"

"Sorry," he said, way too loud right in Lucky's ear.

This was going to be the longest walk of his life.

He started to edge slowly across the hangar toward Jiang's ship with Malby draped over him, one deliberate step at a time, the orb and rifle above his head as the soldiers swiveled their own rifles to follow his path. Lucky could feel their operators measuring up the risk of taking a shot.

"I know we might all die here today," said Jiang over all-comm. "But this may just be the highlight of my life."

In the silence of the cavernous hangar, Lucky could hear three things;

The sound of his and Malby's two-step across the hangar.

The metallic scraping of battle gear as several dozen rifles followed.

And the stifled laughter of Dawson and Jiang.

"I feel there's a dick joke here I'm missing," Rocky added.

"Goddamned Marines," he muttered under his breath.

Five minutes and three-hundred excruciating steps later, he shoved Malby into the second container ship while holding the orb high in the air.

A battle trooper dropped to a knee and swung his barrel across the opening to the ship.

Lucky shoved the barrel of his gun even farther into the orb until he thought the material must surely burst. He again began depressing the trigger.

The trooper hesitated, then slowly stood back and slid his barrel away.

Lucky exhaled.

The buzzing in his head was growing louder. It was getting hard to hear and harder to think.

He felt a red mist floating at the edges of his vision. Something murderous crossed his mind. Having the orb this close for this long was a mistake.

"Rocky, I feel Him. He's close."

He strained to hear Rocky's voice but couldn't make out the words. She sounded so far away.

Malby, Jiang and Dawson were safely ensconced within the rock ore outer shell of the other ship. Nothing he'd seen so far from the Union soldiers suggested they could blast through that. Their energy beam rifles only seemed able to chip away at it. Better than their pulse rifles could muster, but still not enough to dislodge them.

That could change at any moment, however, so they needed to work fast.

All he had to do now was get everyone else over to that other ship, activate it with the orb, and get the hell into the fold and the fuck out of dodge.

"This is going to work," he said over his shoulder, reaching the lip of the mangled ship and backing into it, holding his precious orb out in front of him.

He turned to find Vlad and Nico exchanging angry whispers while Orton lay sprawled on the ground.

Lucky was surprised Orton was still out cold, though he didn't have the high-end biobots the Marines did, just cheap, off-the-shelf crap that civvies got.

Then he looked closer and realized Orton's head was cocked at an unnatural angle.

Broken neck. *How did I miss that earlier?*

Nico and Vlad stopped talking. Vlad looked angry. Nico looked tired.

"I think we can all go as a group this time. If they were going to shoot, they would have done it by now."

Nico was wearing another fix bag on his right foot where his biobots worked furiously to rebuild the lost limb.

"Might be your first jump, rookie, but you already hold a record," Lucky said. "I've never known anyone to lose the same limb twice in a single mission."

Nico flashed him a thin smile. "Thanks."

The kid's eyes were sunken. He looked older. Sounded it, too. A few combat engagements would do that.

"Or just one really screwed-up one," said Rocky.

Lucky doubted he himself looked much better. He was on the upper range of his stimulant cocktail limits. "You got this," he said.

This time Nico didn't smile.

Vlad's eyelids started fluttering again, accessing something in her mind. He knew that as a scientist she had a different data directory from him, but Orton had never done that. In fact, the only other person he had seen do it was—

An explosion boomed, and the ship lurched at a sharp angle.

Lucky felt the orb waver and slip from his grasp.

[42]
INTRODUCTIONS

HE DOVE FORWARD, arms outstretched, his rifle clattering away.

The orb slipped through his fingers, thudded against the floor of the ship, then rolled back into his hands.

He clenched his teeth, waiting for the world to end.

Nothing happened. He exhaled.

And then he was jerked over backward as the floor lurched a final time. This time, it slanted at a hard angle and stayed that way as everything in the small ship shifted to one side.

They slid into a pile at the back of the ship, Lucky comically holding the orb aloft with his outstretched arm.

As the three of them scrambled to their feet, Lucky carefully placed the orb back into the shielded array box in the center of the ship's floor and sighed a heavy but relieved breath.

Poor Orton, he thought, looking at the crumpled body of the scientist. And Cheeky. And Sarge.

What a cluster.

He grabbed his pulse rifle and nodded over at Nico,

who was mobile now though still on one leg. He hopped over to the lip of the ship, bracing his rifle on the edge.

"What the hell's going on, Rocky?"

Rocky sent a drone image into his mind's eye. It was just pulling back from one of the other little ships still cluttering the hangar. As the field of view grew, Lucky's heart sank.

A hole had opened up and swallowed the ship holding Jiang, Dawson, and Malby.

"They blew the floor."

Just like they blew the wall, he thought.

"How did they rig it that fast?"

This whole plan of coming to the hangar had been a disaster. They couldn't have ended up in a worse place if the Union had chosen it.

That thought hung in the air.

He turned to Vlad.

Maybe they had.

"You," he snarled.

She turned as Lucky reached her, and he grabbed her by the throat, slamming her back against the bulkhead.

Someone was going to start paying for this. He needed answers. Now!

"Talk."

But she couldn't talk because Lucky was squeezing her throat so hard she was choking.

He tried to ease back, but he couldn't. The red mist was clouding his vision now.

"No," he whispered. Not here, not now, not yet.

He fought it, fought it with every fiber of his being. Fought Him.

He felt Nico's arm grasp his shoulder, shaking him.

He had to keep The Hate in the bottle. If it got loose here, he would kill Vlad before he got his answers. And he would kill Nico just because. And then he would kill all those Union soldiers up there.

"So, pros and cons," noted Rocky.

The sarcasm worked. He felt the hate ebb. It was Rocky's doing, he knew, but he felt like he had something to do with holding back The Hate.

God I need a drink.

He was finally able to release his grasp on Vlad's throat. She slid down the bulkhead and slumped to her ass.

In the confusion of the melee in his mind, the spiders had gone berserk again. What were they seeing now?

Nico still had his arm on Lucky's shoulder.

"It's okay, I think I have it—"

A fire ignited in his back, blossoming instantly across his entire body. He felt it right down to his dura-alloy skeleton. It burned across his neural network and danced over a trillion nanobots in his bloodstream.

And then he felt nothing.

His body completely rigid.

He sensed his augmented systems were dark. All those Empire goodies that he relied upon so much.

"Rocky?" he tried to echo. It didn't work. Even though it was only ever a mental construct, he could feel the echo connection was gone. His mind's eye was gone.

There was nothing left in his mind but him.

His head hung down. He was drooling.

Then a black combat boot hopped into view. A hand grabbed him by the chin and gently lifted his face.

The sunken eyes of a cool, composed professional killer stood before him.

Nico.

"Hello, Lucky," he said.

Over his shoulder Vlad stood and rubbed her throat, a menacing smile on her face.

She patted Nico on the shoulder, and he stepped aside.

"So you want me to talk?" she said. She nodded at Nico as their eyelids danced in rapid succession. "I'll be happy to."

Lucky heard movement outside. Three union soldiers stepped inside the ship, weapons at their side.

A dozen more loitered outside the ship.

"My name is Do'ock Kun," she said. "But you can just call me Queen Mother." She paused, eyeballing Lucky. "Of the Da'hune."

[43]
FAMILY

The Queen Mother slid the smooth, hard exoskeleton of her talon through a set of quantum beams. She did not understand how her people had devised this. Her clever daughter had explained, and she had nodded along patiently. She looked at her now. She was so smart, so beautiful. She would one day rule the Da'hune, along with her brother, and the elders would bow to them.

But for now the elders were oblivious, like so many on both sides of the Great Corridor.

Soon enough, she thought.

Soon enough, her clan would spill the blood that honor demanded, and they would never again laugh at her for taking the name of the ancient queen of the Da'hune. Her people had lost their way. Her children would return them to the path.

For now, she saw through the eyes of her human surrogate, the one they called Vladlena Alyona.

At long last, they had the key. The gifted one they thought they had lost.

She felt pride for her daughter. Clever Do'ock Kelia. Her

surrogate, Nico, had been brilliant. She had guided the gifted one to the ancient place and kept him safe while they tested the gift.

To see the ancient power harnessed had made her shell quiver. To see how easily the gifted one could navigate the tiny, pathetic corridor the humans had made with their soft, useless hands.

At last, they would traverse the Great Corridor and bring their people home.

Her son entered and showed his fangs to his sister.

He was as brutal as she was cunning.

But both would be needed. One had done her part. Now it was the other's turn.

These are the two minds that a great ruler must know, and that her children must learn.

All rulers sue for peace, but it is won with rivers of blood.

They were coming home to reclaim a universe that had once been theirs, and theirs alone.

Soon, it would be again.

[44]
THE VESSEL

Lucky woke up and just wanted to breathe.

He was drowning. There was green-yellow liquid over his face, filling his eyes, his nose, his mouth.

He tried to reach up, but his hands wouldn't move.

He tried to yell, but his mouth wouldn't open.

He was frozen inside a tank of gel, staring upward into a vast open space.

It was his nightmare, he thought.

He was back in the experiments.

And then Vlad's face appeared floating above him, and he knew it wasn't.

"This must be all too familiar," she said knowingly. "But trust me—this is no dream."

She held an umbilical cord with hundreds of wires wrapped in a fine mesh.

"You say you aren't special just because you lived, but that isn't true, Lucky," she said. "Oh sure, when we first gave you the gift, you weren't special. Just another Empire Marine we captured and experimented on. But then you did something no one else did. You survived. So really, just living is *exactly* what makes you special." She shrugged and paused a moment. "Okay, so the logic is a little circular."

She nodded, and a hand reached down and yanked him out of the goo.

Nico held him aloft with his left hand, a smile menacing.

His right fist smashed into Lucky's face. He heard his nose pop, felt the sensation of blood oozing down his face and over his drooling lips.

Nico hit him a second time. A third. A fourth.

Lucky waited for the stimulants to kick in. For the pain to turn off. For the biobots to stop the blood and heal his nose.

Nothing happened. The pain didn't ebb, and the blood kept flowing.

He realized that he wasn't used to pain, not real pain. He hadn't felt this in years, not since he was in boot—just another grunt without augmented tech.

He felt his mind wandering.

Nico slapped him back.

Vlad stepped up, holding the cord, which Lucky noticed was connected to a curved metallic plate. On the underside of the plate were a dozen long, sharp barbs.

"This might hurt," she said with a grin.

Lucky's eyes bulged, but before he could do anything Nico had wrenched him forward, doubling him over.

A pain unlike anything he had ever felt in his life slammed into the back of his neck as the barbs slide deep into the bottom of his head, forcing his chin into his chest.

He staggered and fell to his knees.

"I understand the grief over your sister, I really do," she said, leaning down and whispering. "Nothing is more important than family. Nothing."

She stood tall. "But if it is any consolation, she would have just died in the experiments like everyone else. Your circumstances were"—she paused again and smiled—"unique."

Vlad glanced at something on her equipment. He couldn't see it, but he was vaguely aware he was on the platform he'd seen from the drones when *Happy Giant* emerged through the corridor.

She came back smiling triumphantly.

"Thank you, Lucky," she said. "Thank you so much."

Lucky saw tears rolling down her cheeks.

"And since you have given me so much, I'm going to give you something in return. I'm going to tell you a story."

"Mother," Nico said, but Vlad held up her hand.

"Compassion follows conquest," she said. "All great rulers must know this."

Nico rolled his eyes.

Vlad turned back to Lucky. Her eyes glazed over, and her eyelids fluttered. Her voice changed, growing deeper and huskier. It was the voice of someone—or something—much larger.

You know of the Da'hune. I know the ship told you of their ancient ways. They were warriors—gods—who purged this universe of all that threatened their offspring, so that they would have a cleansed space in which to grow strong.

And strong they grew. And mighty. But they also grew complacent. And in this fertile soil, a seed of doubt also grew.

And so it came to be that the council of elders decreed that the cleansing had been a mistake.

To rectify this, they undertook the Great Crossing. The ship told you of this, as well, for the passage through the

Great Corridor was what the ship and millions like it were commissioned for.

It was the greatest event in the history of your universe, as it was in the universe they arrived in. A migration that the Da'hune still celebrate today.

They called the new universe home, and set about preparing it for offspring according to the new ways. The council of elders chose to enslave all the peoples they came across in the new universe. Rather than cleansing, they subsumed.

It was folly.

All the rot that the early Da'hune saved their offspring from polluted them now. The Da'hune became twisted and weak. The millions of species in their midst dulled them like sand to an edge.

When they should have turned on those around them, they instead chose to turn on themselves.

And so our universe became engulfed in the endless war, a million-year civil war that could have no victor.

All because of the folly of the Great Crossing.

Only one clan in all the Da'hune saw this folly. Only one clan chose to see the wisdom of the ancients. The mighty Do'ock.

And for that epiphany, they were driven from their homes, forced to live a nomadic life.

They searched tirelessly, generation upon generation, for the fabled Great Corridor, where the ancients had combined their great abilities to find the pathway across the universes. They scoured ancient texts to understand the power the ancients wielded.

And they succeeded.

They found the Great Corridor. They reached across the

plane and found that the desolate universe was not as desolate as fables had told them.

They found weak minds, and with the help of the ancient texts, they learned to invade, overpower, and turn to their own needs.

Through them, they scoured the old universe for all the T'ket'ka they could find and brought them together at the Great Corridor.

They found the ores the ancients used to build their great passage ships and built more of their own. They used the humans to make crude replicas of the ancient corridors.

But try as they might, they could not pass through the Great Corridor.

The T'ket'ka opened the corridors, but inside were all the pathways in all the galaxies in all the universes in all the dimensions that had ever existed or ever would. Those who entered never returned.

They could not decipher how the ancients had used the T'ket'ka. The fables called it the gift, and it was worshiped by the ancients as proof of their divinity.

Even the later Da'hune saw it as more art than science, a melding of technology and intelligence.

And so the Do'ock set about using their human puppets to try to give the gift to humans themselves. They tried experiment after experiment, inserting the gift according to any and every ancient text they could find.

But no matter what they did, the weak-minded humans always rejected the gift.

It was hopeless.

They had all but given up until one surrogate—this one you see before you—learned of a human who had inexplicably survived one of their earliest experiments. There had been a fire. All had perished, or so they thought. This human had somehow managed to escape. He was very lucky indeed.

For five decades, the human was marooned in an escape pod, in hypersleep, alone with the gift.

And then something amazing happened.

The pattern-controlling skills that had killed and maimed and tortured so many other humans took root and blossomed.

That human could read the pathways. He had the gift.

He used the gift carelessly and recklessly in the mundane wars of the humans. But this was understandable, and we have forgiven him. For he did not know, could not know, that the Da'hune had blessed him.

He had been chosen.

He was the vessel.

Vlad's shoulders sagged. Her eyes were bloodshot. A line of blood trickled from her forehead.

Lucky understood now. He had been maneuvered like a piece on a chess board.

The unexplained transfer. The sabotage that isolated them on the planet. The puppets that seemed to miss or hesitate when they had him cornered. The nukes that drove them to the ship.

All to get him to the corridor.

Lucky spat at her feet. "Congratulations for getting me to pass your little test," said Lucky. He pushed his chin up, the pain in his neck blinding as the sharp barbs tore at his flesh. "But I'm sure as fuck not driving your ship."

For a long moment, Vlad said nothing. Then she looked at Nico.

"He still doesn't get it."

"I told you."

Nico mashed his foot into Lucky's back, shoving him forward. His face slammed into the ground. He felt his neck tremble as Nico grabbed a handful of the umbilical cord.

Vlad leaned over until her face was right next to his.

"You were the vessel, asshole. We have what we need."

She stood up and left Lucky reeling.

But he had just flown the ship through the fold, hadn't he?

Hadn't he?

No, he realized. He hadn't. The ship never spoke with him directly.

It always spoke with Rocky. Through Rocky.

And then he heard Vlad's words again: *"The gift is a melding of technology and intelligence."*

Intelligence. Artificial intelligence.

They didn't want him. They wanted Rocky.

[45]
HELPLESS

NICO LAUGHED and yanked the umbilical cord.

Lucky's neck snapped back. Pain screamed into his mind.

For a moment, he thought he'd blacked out.

"Rocky?" he echoed frantically. *"Rocky?"*

Nothing. Nothing at all. The silence frightened him more than anything he had ever felt in his entire life.

Then an explosion rattled his teeth and lifted him into the air.

He watched as the ground and sky flipped around and around.

He landed like a rag doll, facedown and legs folding backward over his head.

Then his weight shifted as he tumbled, and he found himself face-up on his back, staring upward at the cavernous, hollowed-out hangar.

Without Rocky and—he realized now—her gift from the Da'hune, he would soon be dead. His luck had truly run out.

Why had it never occurred to him that he was way too

good at reading patterns? That it wasn't normal to be able to space jump directly at an energy cannon and never get scratched? Or run through a debris field flanked by enemy fire and expect to never take a hit?

But of course it had occurred to him. He had just assumed that Rocky was that good. He just assumed his luck was in having an AI copilot as amazing as Rocky. She was his secret.

And in that sense, he was right.

It was comforting to know. He truly wasn't special. He never had been. Rocky was special. His sister had been special, one of the best pilots in the fleet. His father had been special, the youngest admiral in the fleet.

But he had always just been lucky. And now, he wasn't even that.

Lucky still couldn't move. Whatever they had done to his nervous system to yank Rocky out of him, it had royally screwed him up. And without any biobots to put him back together again, there was nothing he could do but lay there and die.

His head lolled to one side, his neck muscles torn to shreds. He doubted he could raise his head.

He spotted Nico kneeling behind a portion of the ore tower at the far end of the platform. He was firing his pulse punch rifle with perfect technique, keeping his shoulders relaxed and taking short, controlled pulls on the trigger. He rotated on one knee in and out of position behind the edge of the doorway. Swing, aim, squeeze, swing back. Repeat.

Then a chunk of the ore ripped away with a shot, forcing Nico to dive back farther into the structure.

What the hell? No way an Empire pulse rifle could do that to this ore.

And then he saw Jiang. She weaved through equipment

scattered on the platform, then dove behind a support column.

She wasn't holding a pulse rifle. She had one of those badass modified energy weapons.

As he watched, she executed a perfect maneuver, firing on two Union combat troopers running along the top of the tower adjacent to the platform. The energy beam split both in half, their mutilated bodies falling silently, in pieces, off the tower.

Lucky could hardly believe it.

These goddamned Marines, he thought. They came back for me.

How they had managed to fight their way out of that ship with a thousand Union soldiers bearing down on them he couldn't imagine.

Actually, he could. They were Marines.

Jiang looked over at Lucky, and they made eye contact.

"Lucky!" she yelled with a crooked smile. "We couldn't have a party without you. So we brought it with us."

As she said it, Lucky saw movement out of the bottom of his vision, back by the nose of the ship that still sat awkwardly at an angle at the far end of the platform, less than a quarter-klick from the corridor arches. The platform swarmed with Union soldiers pouring from the alien ship.

Now he understood what she meant.

They were outgunned, but they weren't outmaneuvered. They just left those Union dirt eaters in their dust.

The ploy worked wonders tactically, but the number of soldiers was overwhelming.

He tried to call up a drone view out of habit.

A set of black combat boots stepped into his field of view.

Then two more.

Dawson was standing over him, blond hair still showing under the edges of his faceplate, a big smile curling his lips.

"Well, what have we here," he said in his drawl. "I think I recognize this guy."

Next to him, Malby was scowling. "Can he walk?" he asked Dawson, like Lucky wasn't there.

In fact, Lucky barely was there. He was useless as a wet rag.

Malby looked down at him. "Can you walk?"

Lucky wanted to tell him to go to hell.

But he couldn't walk. Or talk. Or even blink.

"Doesn't look like it," Dawson said, bending over him.

Then a pulse hit him in the back, just below his shoulder. He flew over Lucky's head.

"Dammit!" yelled Malby as he dove over Lucky.

A volley of pulses flew over his head while he stared helplessly forward.

And then he saw Dawson, crawling, pulling himself over Lucky.

They locked eyes. Blood seeped out the front of his combat shell. The pulse had gone completely through and burned a hole in his chest.

And then someone jerked Dawson up.

Nico looked down at him with that professional killer expression.

He smiled and stared into Lucky's eyes, and without removing his glare he set the muzzle of his pulse rifle against Dawson's faceplate.

He pulled the trigger, and Dawson's head recoiled, his faceplate absorbing the blow and dissipating energy around the edges.

Nico pulled the trigger again, and Dawson's head bounced and recoiled once more.

He fired again. Dawson's faceplate engineering finally gave up, and a crack appeared.

He fired again, and the crack spidered as more energy couldn't be displaced.

He fired again. Again. Again. Again. Dawson's head kept bouncing back and forth.

The faceplate finally exploded, and metal splayed outward.

Blood splattered down at Lucky's face, and he tasted it on his lips.

Nico's lips curled back in a bigger smile.

Then a pinpoint of light erupted from his shoulder blade, and he howled with pain, spinning away as a blue energy beam sliced horizontally across his arm, nearly severing it. A thick strip of sinew was all that kept it dangling there, combat metal clanking against his side.

He rolled away, stumbling and cursing.

On the catwalk above the platform, Jiang was still firing, teeth gritted, her energy stream following Nico as he scampered away, firing wildly over his shoulder with his good arm.

Then a blast hit the catwalk, and it cracked, threatening to fall backward, then tumbling forward. Jiang was dumped down, flailing as she fell, gun flying. The steel girder collapsed over her.

The impact shook the ground around Lucky, and he slumped again, his weight shifted, and his head flopped over to the other side.

He found himself face to face with Dawson.

Blood oozed from his mouth. One eye was completely red. His blond hair hung out of the broken faceplate, speckled with red spots.

Lucky understood now. All hope was lost.

These Marines had come back for him, and he could only sit, paralyzed, and watch them die right before his eyes.

Dawson had a child somewhere who would only be able to guess at what happened to her father.

Jiang's honor-bound, well-informed family would know how their daughter died, at least, even if it brought them no peace.

Malby was probably hiding somewhere, wondering why the hell he came back. It wasn't because he gave a damn about Lucky.

That made him laugh.

"Who does give a damn about Lucky?" he echoed.

But no one heard him. His mind was empty.

Goddammit, he hated himself. He hated feeling sorry for himself. Hated himself for wanting to give up. Pathetic.

Red clouds began to ring the edges of his vision.

Union soldiers were casually sauntering across the platform now. Mopping up.

He grew more and more angry.

The red clouds in his vision billowed thicker. The world turned a dark, blood-soaked red.

He felt The Hate pulsing inside him.

There was no Rocky in his mind to check it, no way to slow it.

For once, he was glad.

He welcomed it.

[46]
GIVE UP

Hello, Hate.

Hello, Lucky, said The Hate.

He was back in his nightmare.

He was under the tank, where he had crawled as the fire and smoke all around began to choke him.

He felt the pocket of air beneath the tub thinning out.

If the flames didn't kill him, the smoke would.

He tried to reach his AI again, but there was so much static and noise in his head. He could hear a far away voice shouting at him, but strain as he might, he couldn't understand it. Couldn't hear the words.

He tried to give up, but something inside wouldn't let him.

It laughed at him. Mocked him.

It willed him forward in a red cloud of anger and disgust. He saw blood in his mind, felt savage power.

He gave up, and let the seething hatred take over.

It wasn't laughing at him anymore. Now he was laughing. And rising, throwing the tank off.

The Hate jolted him, and he started crawling.

It kicked him and screamed at him with fury.

It directed him.

The Hate knew this place, knew where it was going.

Now he was in front of an airlock. Where did it come from? He didn't know.

Now he was inside a ship. He had never seen it before. But he knew how to operate it.

Now he heard an automated voice, and he fell back.

Now he was speeding away, the symphony of static and noise receding.

Hell was back there, and he didn't even know how he left it behind.

"I have more to cleanse!" screamed a voice in red-hot fury.

He felt his head explode in rage.

Get. Up. Now.

[47]
THE HATE

A DEMON TORE at his flesh, ripping at him from the inside. It was screaming and shaking with rage.

And then he realized it wasn't something the scientists put in him. This wasn't what the experiments of the Da'hune were trying to put in him.

This was what caused the fire and destruction in the lab.

This was what led him out.

He was a chosen one after all. Not chosen by the Queen Mother.

Chosen by The Hate.

Chosen by the cleansing scourge of the ancient Da'hune. The power that they worshipped as divine.

This was The Hate. And it was not a god. It was a demon.

Lucky didn't understand how or why he knew this, but he did.

It survived with the ancient ship. It survived inside the T'ket'ka.

And now it survived inside Lucky.

This was the thing that cleansed the universe of all other life to preserve itself and its own.

This was the essence of the ancient Da'hune.

This killer was inside his head.

He let it out.

[48]
TOO LATE

A Union soldier leaned over Lucky, staring into his face.

Lucky felt his fingers move, causing his breath to catch.

He didn't have his bots or his AI, but whatever had shocked his system was wearing off.

The Hate had chewed right through it.

The Union soldier sensed the change, and tensed.

The Hate slammed Lucky's face forward into the soldier and swung his hand upward, slapping the muzzle of the rifle into the side of the soldier's head. A beam of bright blue light burned the Union soldier's face away, eating his helmet.

Blood dripped onto Lucky's chest plate.

He laughed in a high, angry pitch, howling with delight.

He pulled the body close, using it as a shield.

He grabbed up the energy blaster and began gleefully spewing a single stream of blue energy at the dozens of soldiers on the platform who had foolishly lowered their weapons.

They thought the battle was won.

It wasn't.

Soldier after soldier was sliced in half, folding over in mutilated heaps.

The few who could fire back splattered energy pulses into the heavily armored back of the trooper Lucky held aloft.

He turned as another soldier tried to come from behind him.

He slammed his rifle across his face, then leapt on him.

It was Nico.

A deranged smile crossed Lucky's face.

Nico's eyes grew wide.

Lucky slammed his rifle butt into Nico's faceplate. Again. Again. Again. Again.

It cracked and caved in. Again. Again. Again.

His face was a red pool of bubbling blood, yet still he lashed out.

Again. Again. Again.

The rifle butt was hitting the platform now, nothing solid enough left to slow its momentum.

There were many ways you could wound a Frontier Marine and he would regenerate, but pummeling the organic matter in his brain to mush was not one of them.

He reached down and threw Nico over his shoulder, using him as his new shield as he ran across the platform.

He reached the ore wall and rammed into a soldier coming down the stairs there, grabbing him and twisting and pulling and jerking until his arm came loose from its socket and spun freely from his body.

He swung him over the edge of the stairwell and barreled up into another soldier who was too slow to raise his gun.

He smashed his own gun into his face, using it like a club.

But it wasn't his gun. It was the arm from the other soldier.

He chortled—a deep, mirthful, evil laugh as the blood splattered the walls of the stairwell.

And then he was inside the control tower. And there weren't soldiers here, only people in jumpsuits.

There were screams, and some ran for the door.

Oh no you don't, said The Hate, and it grabbed all that it could reach, clawing at eyes and battering bodies over control panels. He tasted something wet and salty in his mouth.

And then he had his rifle in his hand, and he was beating on something. Screens exploded below his onslaught. Energy seared across the room, bouncing off the walls. He was screaming and smashing and screaming and smashing.

And then he was floating and spinning.

The gravity inside the room was gone.

Bewildered, he didn't know where he was or how he got there.

A faint red cloud faded from the edges of his vision.

He was crying, sobbing uncontrollably.

That meant only one thing. The Hate.

Someone whispered in his ear.

"Rocky?" he cried. "Rocky?"

"It's okay, man," the voice said. "You're ok." It was Jiang.

He lifted his head, and Malby was looking at him, frightened. "Holy hell. I can't even," he said. "I heard rumors, but ... goddammit."

He was floating at the other end of the room they were in.

Lucky realized now it was the control room above the platform.

Dawson pushed off the opposite wall, and Lucky took a double take.

"You're alive," he said.

Dawson turned, keeping his distance from Lucky. His helmet faceplate was cracked and gone, but otherwise his face was fully healed. "Yeah," he said, shaken. "It takes more than a few cheap shots to kill me." But his voice faltered.

He just kept staring at Lucky. They all were.

"Like battering his brain into paste," said Malby, glancing at Lucky.

An image flickered across his mind, a slow-motion replay. He saw what The Hate had done to Nico. What *he* had done to Nico.

He saw other things, too, but he refused to watch more.

Outside the room, he saw the body of a Union soldier gagging and floating, bouncing off the window.

Inside, the control room looked like a war zone.

Bloody bodies were everywhere. Some of them looked like an animal had torn into them. One had its throat ripped open, another was missing an arm.

The equipment was smashed and smoking. Energy sparked and jumped from box to box.

Jiang was looking outside the control room at the chaos on the platform. The artificial oxygen field was lost when the gravity generator stopped. Unlike the Marines, these station troops didn't have airtight suits. Bodies floated off into the larger hangar space to mingle with docked ships and gear.

"You saved us," said Jiang.

Nothing could be further from the truth, thought Lucky.

He couldn't keep the demon at bay now. Not without Rocky.

"No—" he started, then stopped.

Jiang put a hand on his chest plate.

"I understand," she said.

And Lucky realized that she did.

Tears welled up in her eyes. "You can't help it," she said, tears flowing now. "You can't help it."

Lucky dreaded what she was about to say next.

A switch flipped in his head.

He knew the truth.

"I killed your brother."

Lucky felt the air suck out of the room.

Malby and Dawson fell still.

Jiang shook her head. "No," she said firmly, as if convincing herself. "No, It killed my brother."

Oh, god.

Oh, god, no.

"Rocky? Is it true?"

No wonder she wouldn't give him the info on her.

Rocky didn't respond. He'd forgotten again.

Jiang closed her eyes and drew in a long, ragged breath. "I couldn't forgive you for a long time. I thought I knew you. But I guess we always think we know the person we sleep next to better than we really do." A long pause. "But I understand now. About Rocky. About The Hate." She smiled through tears, the saddest thing he had ever seen. "You couldn't help it. I understand that."

The way she kept repeating that made it seem to Lucky like she didn't understand at all.

Lucky wanted to kill himself.

"But I couldn't be near you. You understand that, right? I had to leave. I transferred here to never see you again."

"And yet, here I am," he croaked, feeling tears form in his eyes, too.

"Here you are," she said, the slightest hint of a wry smile at the corner of her mouth. "Saving us all."

"No," he whispered, shaking his head. "Rocky is gone. They took her."

Jiang sat up straighter, her face now a picture of concern.

"I—I can't keep it at bay. Not without her."

"Who took her?"

As if on cue, a long, dark shadow fell across the control room.

One of the modified Union ships glided by. Then another. And another.

"Looks like the party's over," said Malby.

Lucky looked down at the platform. "She's gone," he said.

Happy Giant wasn't on the platform.

"There!" said Jiang, pointing to the far side of the hangar.

A typical spaceport gate lay open, similar to ones the Empire used on their hangars. The ships were flowing through in groups of three.

Happy Giant was already through the gate and out into open space.

"Vlad," said Lucky.

The fleet of Union ships was almost gone now, along with their T'ket'ka orbs.

And Rocky.

"That bitch," said Jiang.

Beyond the gate, something was off.

"What the hell?" said Dawson.

Then it hit him. There were no stars. Just like the small

corridor they had come through. But this wasn't some small patch of space. The complete emptiness covered almost all the sky beyond the hollowed-out hangar.

This *was* the Great Corridor.

"My God," said Jiang. "We're too late."

[49]
OIC

"Good," said Malby, stowing his rifle. "What more can we do? It's not like this hangar isn't still crawling with Union soldiers. So we spaced the ones on the platform. Big deal. Look at this infrastructure."

He pointed to the lattice of scaffolding and control rooms scattered around the outside edges of the hangar, where they reinforced the rock ore shell.

"There're plenty more out there," he said.

He was right. The asteroid was hollow, but it was massive. The infrastructure stretching around the outside of the space was vast.

Then again, this was clearly the central control tower for the dock, and by extension, the entire facility. As long as they could hold this, they were in control of the station.

But the Union would know that, too. And whoever was left that could organize themselves would do so shortly and start an assault on their position.

"What would you suggest we do?" asked Jiang. "Maybe you haven't been keeping up with current events, but they're planning to open up a passageway to another universe."

"So what? It's a big universe. C'mon in!" waved Malby, theatrically.

"Did you see how big that alien ship was? Vlad said they were three times our size," she said. "And they'll be here soon if we don't stop this."

"Exactly. Does an entire race of those things sound like something we should be taking on single-handedly?" Malby looked around at Lucky and Dawson. "Seriously, we can't go chasing a fleet of ships into some black hole in space," he said. Then more to himself, "And chasing them with what? I can't even believe we're talking about this!"

He turned and looked at Lucky expectantly. "Well, sir," he said sarcastically. "What say you?"

Lucky thought for a long moment.

"Can we space jump to that lead ship?" he asked Jiang.

"What?" exploded Malby.

She cocked her head. "We don't have our hammer-heads," she said.

"We don't need to be fast. Those things fly at conventional speeds, and they have no weapons."

"Unless the Union decided to modify theirs to be more offensive," suggested Dawson.

"I can't believe we're talking about this," Malby said again.

Jiang pointed out the control window. "We have all the gear we need."

Lucky nodded. True enough. Union tech was crap, but even they could make decent hammerheads. Just point in the direction you want to go, and jump. They weren't technically made for space-to-space jumps, but he'd done it before. They had enough maneuvering thrusters to make it work.

"No, no, no, no!" fired Malby. "We need to regroup. We need to make contact with HQ. Am I the only one here who ain't crazy? Dawson?"

Dawson reluctantly turned to Lucky. "The spirit is willing and all," he said, "but ... Malby has a point."

"Thank you!" yelled Malby, face and palms upward.

Lucky took a deep breath. He was so tired. Something about the Hate had juiced his biobots, but that was wearing off fast. The Hate didn't care about pain and suffering. It didn't dodge damage, it dove headfirst into it. And now Lucky was paying the price.

"I understand where you guys are coming from," he said at last. "I got the inside scoop on the hell coming our way. You didn't."

"Suffice it to say," he said, looking at Dawson, "Your child will never grow up to live a happy life. This will consume our universe from now until the end of time."

Dawson said nothing, but tightened his grip on the barrel of his pulse rifle. The smile slowly faded.

"Malby, I'm not going to argue with you," he said. "I don't know why the hell you came this far, but those mistakes have already been made, son." He closed his eyes and laughed. *"How's my inspirational speech going so far?"* he echoed.

No response.

Oh right. Damn.

Malby looked around. "I can't believe this. He's crazy. You get that, right?" He looked at Jiang. "Fubar in the head."

"You once told me I didn't look so tough," said Lucky. "Do you remember that?"

Malby frowned. "Yeah, well. Okay, so, I was wrong about that."

"No, you were right. I'm a coward," he said. He motioned to the room. "Killing is easy. I love a good fight because I know I can win."

He thought about Rocky and her spiders. He thought about The Hate.

"But when I have to make a tough call, I put my tail between my legs," he said. "When it's hard, I run."

Malby said nothing.

"I wish to God that Sarge were here," Lucky said. "That someone else was here in charge. I wish it was anyone but me." He closed his eyes. "But it's time for us to stop being cowards, Malby," he said. "You and me. We're Marines, and we don't quit when everything goes tits up. We go to work."

"I'm no coward," Malby said under his breath.

Lucky opened his eyes and looked at him. "Well, you should at least be scared right now, asshole." Lucky spread his arms wide. "You are standing in the presence of the most dangerous thing in any universe," he said. "The officer in charge."

Dawson rolled his eyes.

Jiang had a big grin on her face.

Malby just shook his head. "Except, of course, you aren't an officer."

"He's got you there," Jiang said.

"Fine, I'm the highest-ranking member in charge. Happy?"

"No," said Malby.

Lucky ripped his punch pistol from his holster. "I could just shoot you then."

Malby's eyes got big as saucers.

Dawson and Jiang exchanged glances.

Then Malby burst out laughing. "You are one crazy son of a bitch, you know that, Lucky?"

Lucky put his pistol away. "You don't know crazy yet."

Lucky edged himself over to an undamaged console on the opposite side of the control room. He might not have had Rocky, but these control stations were pure old-school Union tech, something the operators could handle. And so could he.

"I have a plan," he said. "A very, very, very bad plan."

"I like it already," said Jiang.

[50]
ALMOST

DO'OCK KUN, Queen Mother of the Da'hune, stood inside the control room of her flagship battlecruiser.

Her tail swished along with the others in the cramped quarters.

Her clan deserved better for this momentous occasion. Perhaps the historians would be kind. She chided herself. Of course they would be. What kind of ruler would she be if she didn't write her own history?

But this was what she could spare—a mere ten thousand ships from her million-strong Do'ock fleet. The endless war must be fed, even when the Do'ock would soon end it with their glorious return to their rightful home.

And she certainly didn't need the firepower. She had seen enough of the humans to know that! She worried only for posterity. Her children must know that a ruler's power flows through the perception they foster in their subjects.

She stroked the shell of her firstborn, her lovely, clever Do'ock Kelia.

She had been forced to relinquish her surrogate, Nico.

But no matter. Do'ock Kun would soon shed her surrogate as well.

She looked down at her brutal son, Do'ock Nigh'tok. The ferocious snarl was sweet suckle to her soul. He had the spirit of the ancient ones. The purge harkened back to their ancient gods, and she saw divinity in her son's vicious savagery.

The Queen Mother once more slid the smooth, hard exoskeleton of her talon through a set of quantum beams.

She was impatient, checking the progress of her surrogate.

But in truth, it was something more. Her surrogate Vlad was the vessel for the gift now. It resided in her, and by association, Do'ock Kun sensed she could feel its power as well. She doubted this was true, but she did not want to ask. She would rather be ignorant and bask in ancient art. Her shell trembled. She could feel it, she was sure!

She closed her eyes now and saw through her surrogate's eyes as she rushed onward, into the Great Corridor.

How pleasant to see it from the vantage point of the other universe, to know what lay just ahead of her.

The distributed human-made ships were fanned out across the corridor, their precious T'ket'ka orbs creating a halo of protection into which her brutal son would soon guide their ships.

Almost there ... Her surrogate was peering at something, and it caught the Queen Mother's eye as well.

She leaned in, willing her surrogate to do the same.

Something was trailing behind her.

Something huge.

[51]
A PLAN

"I HAVE to stop supporting your plans before I see them," said Jiang.

"It's a good plan," he said.

"It's a plan," she responded.

Lucky fired a stream of blue energy across space into the edge of the hangar's gateway, destroying the mechanism and locking it in place as they passed through.

He looked down the alien-infused Union rifle and nodded approvingly. A nice upgrade.

"Everybody remember where we're parked," Dawson said, as the space jumpers emptied the firing rockets on the Union hammerheads and screamed out of the hangar at top speed, adding their own rocket burn to the ever-increasing speed of the asteroid itself.

Lucky felt his pack pull slightly starboard and compensated. *The Union can't even make hammerheads that worked right,* he thought. Old Union tech was still just old Union tech.

The new stuff that Da'hune helped them with, on the other hand, was a different story.

He glanced back over his shoulder. It wasn't every day that you saw a spaceport carved into a hollowed-out asteroid.

It was even less often you saw it under power.

Even with the push, though, *Happy Giant* and the other alien ships were just tiny pinpoints again the vast, complete black canvas of the Great Corridor.

Without the drones, Lucky didn't any have technical data to review.

"Are we going to catch them?"

"It'll be close," said Malby. "We should get there right when they do."

That was too close. If they weren't tight enough to the ships and their T'ket'ka when they hit the corridor, they would never enter the fold. They would just sail right through.

A dozen drones flew a tight formation around the Marines. Without Rocky, Lucky couldn't control his, but he wasn't sure he had any left to control anyway.

They had started this mission with a thousand drones per Marine. Then again, *we started this mission with a hell of a lot more Marines,* he thought.

Then he almost ended up next on the dead list.

Something fast screamed overhead, and he saw the other Marines scatter. Without an AI link, he got no warning.

"Skreamers!" shouted Jiang.

Lucky rolled to his right and directly into a stream of blue light. He would have been sliced in half—should've been—but a rogue locust made the same poor choice he had, and it exploded in his face on impact with the beam, causing a reaction from Lucky that sent him barrel-rolling in the other direction.

"Dawson called it!" said Malby.

"Not quite," he said, his drawl casual despite their predicament. "I thought they'd add defenses to the ships, not fill them with skreamers."

"Same difference," said Malby.

"Dive fast, Marines!" said Jiang, as she nosed down harder.

They all did the same, but Lucky felt blind without a drone view.

The skreamers flipped in unison and started coming back around now, but they were having trouble lining them up.

They couldn't fly slow enough to get a good shot on the jumpers. Perhaps the only advantage they had was that they were so inconsequential that the skreamers were having trouble swatting them out of space.

Three of the skreamers joined together in tandem, cutting at different angles as they dove, keeping the energy streams flowing throughout the maneuver. The result was a grid of blue energy that sliced through the tight formation of diving Marines.

Lucky felt desperately for his spiders to pluck at his mind, knowing it was irrational.

"Lucky, look out!" screamed Jiang.

He pulled up, hoping it was the best option, not having drone data to reference.

He chose poorly.

A pop and explosion from his back told him he had maneuvered right into an energy arc.

He heard a sizzle and crack from his hammerhead pack.

The hammerhead saved his life, but now it flopped and bounced off his back, one of the thrusters badly damaged.

The pack compensated with the other thruster, and he found himself flying at an odd angle.

He immediately started to fall back from the others.

Jiang flared her arms and settled back with him.

"No!" he screamed. "No slowing down."

A moment later, another beam of blue energy shot across their position.

Before it could hit either of them, a drone appeared and dived into it, sparking an explosion but taking the brunt of the blow. That was the second time a drone had saved his life on this jump—and it gave him an idea.

"You guys head for the ship," he said. "I'm going to cover you."

"You're gonna do what?" Jiang asked.

"You aren't exactly in tip-top shape," said Malby.

"This is all taking too long," he said. "We have to make that window, otherwise we miss the corridor completely. You guys have to keep burning at max."

"Never stopped, chief," said Malby. "No offense."

"Just be ready to come get me," he said, nodding at Jiang before flipping himself over. It was a tough move with his hammerhead thrusters off balance, but it got him more or less facing the right direction.

He looked over at Jiang, who still hadn't re-engaged her thrusters.

"Seriously, this will work," he said. "I learned it from an old friend."

At last, she pulled away.

This will never work, he thought.

[52]
FLIGHT TIME

The drones had given him the idea.

Of course, they had died for their trouble.

But The Hate had taught him it would work.

When in doubt, attack.

He rocketed directly at the nose of a skreamer. Even with only one thruster, his closing speed was enormous. What he needed was for it to—

The skreamer flipped for another run, dropping all speed, before accelerating again. The pause was all Lucky needed.

He smashed headlong into the side of the skreamer, his single thruster flaring at maximum speed at the last second, doing nothing to soften the blow but ramming him up to a high enough velocity to get his finger on the lip of its front plate assembly as it started away again.

He felt his fingers pulled and ripping, sensed that the O-ring on his combat suit was failing.

In his mind, he could hear Rocky telling him all about it while his biobots came running to save the day.

But none of that happened. He jerked at the Union rifle

still holstered inside the leg of his left combat boot. It didn't fit like his own rifle had, and now the damned thing wouldn't come loose!

His fingers were growing numb now. He couldn't feel anything below his wrist.

He yanked and yanked, but still the rifle wouldn't budge. Belatedly, he realized the oversize rifle was caught in the edge of his hammerhead assembly.

He kicked out with his leg, bouncing the assembly loose and yanking the pulse rifle out in one motion.

Unfortunately, the jostling dislodged the deadened hand that had been holding him to the skreamers front plate assembly.

As he slid down, he found himself spread eagle over the cockpit window. A pilot in black Union gear stared at him in shock.

Lucky slapped the muzzle of the rifle against the cockpit window and pulled the trigger.

At the same moment the pilot snapped loose his restraints and ducked as far forward as he could go.

The blue beam shattered the edge of the cockpit, ripping it open, and sliced a hole in the top of the seat where the pilot's head had just been.

A release of oxygen exploded in Lucky's face, and he should have been launched into space. But the hand with the broken O-ring saved him again, lodging against what was left of the cockpit window.

Instead, the force of the air blast slammed him against the side of the fuselage.

He swung back around, bringing his arm up for another shot at the pilot.

But the pilot was gone. The cockpit was empty.

He looked back and saw the pilot flailing off into space,

having been sucked out with the expulsion of air.

Probably should have left that restraint on, he thought.

He scrambled into the cockpit, his useless right hand no help.

If this had been an Empire fighter, he would know right where to find the seal kit. But he didn't see anything that looked like it, and he didn't have time to dig around.

This is all taking too long, he thought. *Way too long.*

He turned the skreamer hard right, amazed at the fast response, and remembered that it was Da'hune-influenced tech. It was a dream to fly.

A half-dozen more skreamers were inbound, but they had no idea he wasn't on the same team.

The slow approach to the jumpers meant the fighters couldn't do their normally precise, organized approaches, so all the excitement with his ship hadn't been noticed.

He lined up behind three skreamers that were about to try the same energy beam pattern trick again.

He pulled the trigger on the stick, expecting to see ordnance fly or feel some resistance. But it was complete silence, complete stillness. There was no physical response on the stick or in the ship's framework. Two streams of blue energy simply raced out from the wing tips and sliced the lead ship in half as if it was made of paper. It caught the wingtip of his wingman and sent him spiraling off.

The third skreamer realized the problem, but he was too late. He tried to bug out and up, but Lucky easily matched the maneuver and again depressed the trigger to watch the silent slicing in half of his opponent.

He turned back and found he now had the full attention of the other skreamers, who'd broken off their attack runs on the jumpers and now focused only on him.

"I'm Tango 10 from intercept!" Malby called out.

Ten seconds from arriving alongside the ancient ship.

"You should be able to get back in the way we did before," Lucky said over his all-comm.

He dove into the group of skreamers that were coming at him, getting inside their energy beams, playing chicken. He rolled off hard, bringing two fighters onto his tail while positioning two more in his sights.

"Negative," said Malby.

"The access ports," said Jiang, who was still some ways behind Dawson and Malby. "For the smaller ships that we were on. When they blew the floor, they blew those open. I know they still are—"

"Affirmative!" said Dawson.

"Bingo!" said Malby.

Lucky depressed the trigger on his stick and watched his energy bolt slice across the wingtip of one skreamer. But as he did it, one of the two behind him fired beams of their own. One flew harmlessly high and wide. But Lucky knew with two wingtip shots that the other would—

He felt his plane slide sideways. It didn't stop its forward motion so much as shift into two pieces moving in the same direction. His skreamer began toppling end over end, but it was headed in the direction he wanted to go.

Unfortunately, he was now a big fat easy target. The other skreamer was lining up a run at him.

Now or never, he thought.

He pulled the eject bar and felt the entire cockpit assembly propel forward. He pulled his punch pistol out with his good hand and fired four energy punches against the cockpit supports, separating them.

He holstered the pistol, released his restraints, and shoved off the ejection seat with his feet with all his might.

He drifted downward toward *Happy Giant* while the

cockpit assembly was shoved away from him in the opposite direction.

Heat seared behind him as the cockpit assembly was sliced in half by an energy beam from the skreamer who'd hit him. He doubted they could make out his single signature, especially as they were getting close to the fleet of ships now, but even if they could, they wouldn't be able to get a bead on him for another pass or two.

"Guys, I think I could use that help right about now," said Lucky.

His badly damaged hammerhead had nothing left to give in the way of thrust.

Over his comm came only static.

I missed it, he thought.

[53]
STRANGER

At least they made it. That was the important—

Jiang slid up beside him, and his head jerked around so fast he heard her stifle a laugh.

"You rang," she said, grabbing him by his crippled hand.

He barely concealed a yelp of pain. "Other hand, please," he said through clenched teeth.

She switched over and pulled him down toward the access point to the small hangar full of little giants where they had earlier battled the Union soldiers.

"Back to the scene of the crime," he said, feeling his energy sapping away.

Jiang looked concerned. "Lucky, stay with me," she said.

"What's the problem?" said Malby.

Lucky spotted him and Dawson standing at the port entrance.

"He doesn't have any bots, that's the problem. His damage is adding up."

"No way," said Malby, somehow fascinated by the revelation.

"Not good," said Dawson, looking at Lucky as he pulled him inside the hangar space.

He slapped a med-pack on his wrist, but Lucky was so cold he tried to pull it back off.

"He's not going to make it," Dawson said. "We're in vacuum here. His seals are broken, his faceplate's cracked, not to mention the radiation exposure. He won't last another five minutes."

"Dammit, don't say that," barked Jiang, looking around for inspiration.

"If we could get his biobots working again ..." said Malby, but he trailed off. He was a technical specialist, but even he didn't know how to jumpstart a dead AI.

"It's okay," said Lucky, shocked to hear his voice was just a whisper. "The plan is still a go," he said. "Get moving. I—"

He looked over Malby's shoulder. Similar to the ship's eye that Rocky had shown them in the larger hangar, an image was coalescing inside the smaller hangar. Why would that be active here?

As he watched, two balls were forming and then slowly lowering down to a section of exposed metal near the base of one of the smaller ships.

The ship was one of the few in the hangar that hadn't sustained any real damage in all the fighting earlier.

As Lucky watched, a metal rod with several pins on it detached from the port it was sitting in and slid down toward Lucky.

The balls from the ship's eye settled just below the erect rod. The rod began to bounce a little, and the balls bounced along with it.

Lucky closed his eyes and laughed. "Such a pervert," he croaked, shaking his head.

Dawson, Malby, and Jiang all followed his gaze.

Only Malby caught on and immediately guffawed.

"So lemme get this straight," he said to Lucky. "Your AI is a chick who likes dirty jokes?" he said in astonishment. "Un-goddamn-believable."

Lucky opened his eyes. "You can try your lame pick-up lines on my forehead later. Right now, help me up."

Malby dragged Lucky over to the rod.

Up close, it looked menacing.

"You sure about this?" Malby asked.

"Sadly, yes," he said. Lucky knew it was the pin contacts on the end that mattered.

She could get into him from anywhere inside the ship as long as she had direct access to his neural pathways.

"This is going to hurt," he said. "This is really going to hurt."

He balled up his fists and clenched his teeth.

With the last of his strength, he slammed his neck backwards into the rod, feeling a bolt of searing pain as the metal contacts dug deep into the bloody sore that still hung open on his neck from where Rocky was first torn out of him.

An instant later, the pain was gone. Stimulants hit his bloodstream. His biobots awoke from their slumber, and the dull pounding sensation in his pain receptors receded.

Spiders danced in his mind.

"Hello, stranger," cooed Rocky.

[54]
USELESS

LUCKY SMILED THINLY. *"I thought I'd—"*

"Stow the wet kisses," she echoed. Rocky paused, and Lucky guessed she was connecting with the other Marine AIs.

"You have the plan?"

"Yup."

"Can you guide them?"

"Already done. Their drones have the coordinates."

"Plan hasn't changed," he said to the Marines, realizing he was sounding a lot like Sarge. "And time is getting very, very tight."

"You think?" said Malby. "In case you didn't notice, we're already in the corridor."

"Well, then you'd better hope it lives up to its moniker," he said.

Malby furrowed his brow.

"Great," said Lucky, making air quotes with his hands. "As in 'Great Corridor.' As in very large. As in—"

"Oh my God!" Jiang broke in. "Can we just go?"

"You coming?" said Dawson.

Lucky jerked his head forward, felt the tearing of the metal pins from his neck, and suppressed a scream. The biobots were already plugging away at it, along with everything else, but there was enough here to take time. He gently slid over on his side.

"I'll just sit here and regenerate if it's all the same to you," he said. "I'd be useless in a fight."

"Figures," Malby said under his breath.

Jiang, Dawson and Malby took off at a fast, low run, a gaggle of drones in their wake.

Lucky watched them go.

"You want the bad news or worse news?" echoed Rocky.

"Bad."

"I didn't just mosey on out of Vlad's mind. I had to fork my own source," she said. She paused to laugh at her own phrasing.

Lucky sighed. Had he really wanted this back so bad?

"She still has a full copy of my spiders in her neural system. We have to physically take that back out of her."

"Like they did to me?"

"Exactly."

"Will she know? That you forked out of her?"

"Yes. Even if she didn't, the Ship would tell her. It must honor the gift-holder."

Great.

"And the worse news?" he asked.

"She's using all the other ships in a huge, networked array of T'ket'ka that Vlad is controlling."

Lucky's forehead creased.

"Why do they need all that?"

"Because she isn't going to go through the corridor. She's going to sit here and hold the door open."

"For what?" he asked, then immediately regretted it.

"The ten thousand Da'hune battleships that are entering from the other side. And they are a lot bigger than Happy Giant.*"*

Lucky closed his eyes and tried to imagine that. As usual, his imagination failed him.

But then he smiled. They were holding the corridor open. This meant his plan would work even better—

"Back to the scene of the crime," said a voice that made Lucky gnash his teeth.

Vlad.

And she stole his line.

Lucky dragged himself around the side of the small ship, then his spiders jerked him back. A blast sent part of the ore splintering away.

"You are too late, you know," she said. "So very, very late."

Lucky slammed his head back.

If he could kill her, blow away the AI in her mind, would the T'ket'ka fail? Somehow that seemed too easy.

But he really wanted to kill her.

Lucky slid his rifle into the crook of his left arm. He was in no shape for this. He could still barely stand.

"Rocky? How long to full regen?"

"Ten minutes. But you are ambulatory. That was priority."

In other words, he could run for it. Or stroll very quickly for it, at least.

He looked again at the small hangar. It was just as they had left it. The wall toppled over the wrecked small ship, debris strewn everywhere. A huge hole to his left where the Union had blasted away the floor.

"Rocky, tell me that you still have—"

"On it."

A lone locust slipped out of one of the ships.

Lucky heard the drone fire and leapt out from behind the ship in the same instant. He felt his spiders pluck his mind, and he shifted his weight just as an arc of energy flew past his flank, singeing the side of his combat gear.

The drone was already a fireball drifting away.

"That was close!"

"She has spiders, too," Rocky shot back.

Of course. The pattern-recognition abilities that the Da'hune passed to him were now in her.

Lucky realized this was at best a stalemate. She didn't have his weapons training, but she also didn't have his wounds.

He leapt up again, squeezed off two shots, felt his own spiders jump, and followed their lead.

Vlad jumped away from his shots as he skipped away from hers.

They might be shooting at each other for hours at this rate.

Then a series of explosions erupted in front of him, centered on Vlad.

Jiang, Malby and Dawson were holding defensive positions at the far end of the hangar, lighting up Vlad with pulse after pulse.

Vlad skipped away like a prize-fighter, dipping and juking, rolling away from shot after shot. She fired off one round. Then another. And another.

Dawson fell back, but Jiang and Malby kept alternating shots.

Jiang flipped her rifle and launched a pulse pounder, then flipped it back and dove away.

Vlad laughed playfully, dancing and backtracking her way out of the hangar. The explosion should have killed her, but somehow she managed to contort her body so that the shrapnel flew harmlessly by.

A real lucky move.

"Goodbye, Lucky," she said as she casually stepped out of the hangar. "And thank you again."

Lucky didn't go after her.

Instead, he ran to the next little giant he saw that wasn't damaged. The Marines joined him, Malby keeping his rifle trained on the path Vlad had used while Jiang helped Dawson carry a gear bag.

"I really want to dust that bitch," Malby said.

Lucky nodded. "Join the club."

Jiang gave Lucky a thumbs-up as they dove in. "Time to go," she said.

Dawson set down the gear bag and lifted out a beige orb that throbbed with energy.

"Rocky told our drones right where to find it," he said. "But man, it gives me the heebie-jeebies."

Lucky placed it carefully in the shielded holder in the center of the floor. He felt an instant shift in the small craft as it lifted off the ground.

"*We are gone,*" said Rocky.

The small ship leapt out of the open port in the side of *Happy Giant* and into space.

[55]
FOOLISH

The Queen Mother watched smugly through the eyes of her surrogate as the tiny craft fled the ancient Da'hune ship. Where are you running off to, my little humans? Back to the safety of your universe? Back to the safety of your weak, useless human clans?

So foolish. Their existence was but another example of the wisdom of the ancients. They would never have allowed such beings to pollute their offspring. The purge was natural and right for these creatures. It would be a divine sin not to show them to their end. They were doing them a favor that they couldn't hope to repay.

Her surrogate was in place now. She had laboriously aligned the T'ket'ka. The corridor was open.

She opened her eyes and returned her focus to the control room of her battlecruiser.

She placed a talon on the shell of her brutal son, and he spat furiously at the navigator.

Her clever daughter swished her tail approvingly.

She began to move her forces through the Great Corridor. They were going home.

[56]
INCOMING

LUCKY FELT the small ship straining as it swung upward and away from *Happy Giant*.

The Great Corridor seemed to have a gravity well of its own now, with so many ships and T'ket'ka inside its walls of endless pathways spanning all the universes in all the dimensions that had ever existed.

Or was it all the dimensions in all the universes that had ever existed?

He'd have to leave this one to the eggheads.

Lucky could not fathom the architects of such a thing, and at this moment he only wanted to get away from it as fast as he could.

But the little giant was no different to its bigger sibling. It too was slow and defenseless.

It was, at least, spacious. Which was another terrifying reminder of the architects of the Corridor. The Da'hune were giants.

This was a single-occupant ship if Vlad was to be trusted on the subject, and the four Marines fit comfortably inside with room to spare. Lots of room to spare.

And then he imagined The Hate flowing through them. Not a pretty picture.

"Lucky, I know more about The Hate than I have told you."

Lucky thought for a moment on that. He knew a lot more about The Hate now as well.

"I think a frank discussion might be in order, but it's not like—"

"Skreamers," interrupted Rocky.

"Incoming," he said to the other Marines. The few locusts they had left hugged the side of the little giant. An image floated up in his mind's eye.

A handful of skreamers were coming up fast from below them.

"Never mind," said Rocky.

Never mind? Then he saw it in his mind's eye.

Above them, looming impossibly large, was a massive asteroid falling at breakneck speed down upon them.

The massive Union hangar was caught in the gravity well of the Great Corridor, moving faster even than the Da'hune technology would attempt to accelerate it.

"Here we go," he said, nodding at Dawson.

Dawson opened his gear bag and pulled out the other orb. "Is this going to work?" he asked.

"Damned if I know," he replied. "But it'll be one hell of a show."

[57]
NUDGE

The Queen Mother's battleship led her forces through the Great Corridor.

For a moment, Do'ock Kun closed her eyes and had the sensation of watching her own passage through the eyes of her surrogate.

What a wonder to behold! The moment that would be remembered by her clan for all eternity.

She opened her eyes, eager to experience her new home with her own senses.

Her tail stopped swishing. She raised a talon to the viewport.

What is this, my child?

The navigator did not respond.

Her majestic view of the great expanse was blocked by a large asteroid tumbling down into the corridor, blocking their path.

It was the same one that had been following her surrogate when she first entered the corridor.

It seemed as if this whole time it had continued its slow, spiraling approach.

At this range, she realized what it was. The humans' station, the one they had helped them build and used to make their corridor-crossing ships.

Why it was here now she hadn't a clue. But no matter. It was no longer needed.

She looked down at her brutal son, Do'ock Nigh'tok.

He knew what she was going to ask, and he relished it.

He was so proud of the purge, she thought, so bloodthirsty. And she was so proud of him.

But something was nagging at her mind. She was as ready as her son to start the purge, but she had a vague uneasiness about beginning it here, at the edge of the corridor.

She slid her underbelly talon across his shell.

We shall just nudge it back out of the corridor, she explained. Then, once it has been turned back, you may clear our view of it so that we may lay our eyes on our new home.

He snarled.

Patience, my brutal one, my Do'ock Nigh'tok. The rivers of blood will flow soon enough.

She nodded to their gunner, and he turned to his instruments.

[58]
LONG SHOT

THE LITTLE GIANT leapt through the open gateway.

Even with the relative slowness of the small ship, the speed of the asteroid falling into the corridor meant that everything flew past in a blur.

No ship would ever approach at this speed.

Lucky closed his eyes and relied on Rocky's view in his mind.

It was her show now, but really, it was the spiders.

The Union soldiers had abandoned the hangar, but not before leaving them a nasty surprise.

A pair of cannon batteries placed on the remains of the badly damaged platform erupted, spewing streams of blue energy at them.

The spiders danced wildly on their web, and Rocky obliged, swinging the less-than-nimble craft from port to starboard and back again, then rolling into the sights of the cannons.

The cannons sat between them and the corridor at the end of the platform.

The pitch-black opening was still there, still framed by a

giant arch of gray ore inscribed with alien script.

He felt the spiders in his mind begin to leap about, excited at the streams of data reaching out to them from the fold.

The cannons belched up more fire, and Rocky spun the ship in a tight corkscrew.

"Do it, do it now!" Lucky screamed.

A single locust peeled away from the hull of the ship, falling lazily toward the interior wall of the platform. It released the small beige orb it had been holding. A tiny bolt of energy pulsed from the locust, barely enough to break human skin—but more than enough to pierce the antimatter skin of the T'ket'ka orb.

Rocky held the ship in its tight corkscrew, diving forward, a pattern of increasingly complex lines forming in Lucky's mind.

His spiders were rapturous.

A pinpoint of light flashed behind the ship, washing over it and bathing the hollow asteroid in red flames.

The hollowed-out asteroid was the perfect kindling for the antimatter fire.

Lucky felt the hungry fire reaching out for them.

Closer.

And closer, still.

We timed it wrong, he thought. It was coming for them.

It was always going to be the tightest of windows, the longest of long shots.

But even as the fire reached out to grab them, he felt the spiders reaching forward, pulling out strands of energy and wrapping the small ship within them.

The cocoon of energy could hold back the flames for just a single fleeting moment, but that was all the little giant needed to slip into the corridor.

[59]

KINDLING

The Queen Mother watched as the asteroid erupted in flame.

She turned angrily on the gunner, but he was staring in disbelief.

She looked to her brutal son, seeing in this a lesson in how a ruler deals with insubordination. This was a teaching moment, she thought, but he was staring in disbelief as well. She followed his talons and saw what he saw.

The gunner had not fired.

She looked back now at the asteroid engulfed in flame. It was spreading fast, too fast. Unnaturally fast.

Before her very eyes, she watched as it began to disappear. Once matter, but existing no longer.

She realized what was happening.

"Back!" she screamed to her navigator. "Back!"

But the flaming remains of the asteroid kept falling toward them, shedding matter as it came. And then a tenuous finger of fire reached out, probing the deep. It brushed against the battlecruiser, and a pinpoint of light blossomed.

Another finger reached out to another of her clan ships. And another.

The Queen Mother watched as her mighty flotilla, the great hope for her clan, the bringer of purity to the ancient universe, disappeared before her eyes. Their great mass was now their great flaw. The hungry antimatter clamored over and through them, hungry for more, never sated.

A dull realization fell over her. This would ignite the entire network of T'ket'ka lining the endless paths of the Great Corridor.

Where will it stop? How far must the hunger travel before it is satiated? How deep will the wound go? The ancient power to hold the energy of the corridor was now turning on the very fabric of its own making, doing untold damage to both.

And then Do'ock Kun, Queen Mother of the Da'hune, watched her lovely, clever daughter, Do'ock Kelia, and her bold, brutal son, Do'ock Nigh'tok, burn away before her eyes.

The future rulers of the mighty Da'hune were lost to its ancient power.

And then her own queenly flesh joined theirs.

[60]
CHOSEN

HELLO, nightmare.

Hello, Lucky, said his nightmare.

Lucky awoke in an escape pod.

He didn't know how he got there.

He was in a hyperspace sleeper unit.

He didn't know how he got in it.

How much time had passed?

The timer in the sleeper pod read: 51/Y/38/D/08/H/14/M/

It must be wrong. Everything was covered in ice crystals.

He heard a voice in his head. A red cloud hung at the edge of his vision.

It was a whisper. He strained to hear it.

It was garbled and weak.

"Chosen," it whispered again. And then nothing.

What could that have been? he wondered. He waited and listened, but the voice did not return.

The red mist receded from the edges of his mind.

And then a new voice erupted in his head, fully formed.

"What the hell was that?" it said.

He knew her. They had been talking, he realized. While he slept. How long had it been? A few hours? A few days? Nothing longer than that, surely.

And then a final voice, this one from outside his mind. He had forgotten voices existed outside his mind.

"We got somebody alive here!"

Goodbye, nightmare.

Goodbye, Lucky. For now.

[61]
NEW SIT

WAKE UP, Sleeping Ugly. This cycle is too short even for your shitty meat to get freezer burned, so you should remember all of this, but I doubt it. The brass wants your memory intact so you can explain yourself or something. You're welcome.

[BEGIN SITREP]

Two weeks ago

You, Private First Class Jiang, Private Dawson, and Private Malby, all returned through the Union-made test corridor just before you managed to roast an alien invasion from a parallel universe. Remember that? Good times. An Empire special-ops team picked you up and popsicled you and sent you on your merry way.

Three days ago

You rendezvoused with the main strike force. You were scheduled for thaw there, but some of the brass wanted a look at you in person. Get ready to wake up to generals poking you. Try not to be an ass.

Eight hours ago

The rest of your crew was thawed for debrief. You were not. Personally, I think they are going to hang something on you, but I'm the paranoid type. Comes from living in your head.

Now

Tactical debrief time. Try not to embarrass yourself. Wakey wakey.

[END SITREP]

Lance Corp. Lucky Lee Savage awoke from hypersleep like he had 157 times before.

He didn't know this yet. He didn't know anything yet.

He began his waking cycle the way he always did. Floating inside his mind, drowning, grasping for any thought, any detail—anything—that swirled toward him.

He was a Frontier Marine.

He was a planetary submission specialist.

He hated everyone.

He needed a weapon in his hand.

There he was.

Lucky opened his eyes and winced as bright light bled around the hatch of the sleeping pod.

He wasn't in a recovery room. He was in a hospital room. He knew the smells and sounds immediately. The curved walls suggested a standard medical ship. The medtech insignia on the nurse standing over him cinched it.

"Observant," said Rocky.

"Out of my thoughts, please."

"Trying. Believe me."

Three men in military uniforms stepped up to the side of the pod as the nurse stepped back.

All old, all scowling, and all generals.

"This should be fun," echoed Rocky.

"I'd salute, but ..." said Lucky, noting his hands were still held in the pod restraints.

"I'm Brigadier General Lewis," said the officer to his right. "This is—"

"Can we not, Tim?" cut in the officer on his right.

Four stars. It suddenly dawned on him who he was looking at.

Commandant Apollo.

"We have a very good tactical understanding of what happened, Lance Corporal," said the other general.

Lucky noted he didn't bother introducing himself, or glancing over at the others when he spoke for them, even though he was outranked.

There was something familiar about his condescending tone. Lucky uttered a fleeting laugh. *What if this is Orton's old man?* Then he thought about what that would mean and his mirth melted away.

Lucky found himself replaying the last few hours in his head. Even after a two-week freeze, he felt sluggish.

Then he realized no one was talking.

"I'm not sure what I can add, then," he said.

"They're fishing for something," said Rocky.

"I'm paranoid enough without your help."

"What do you know about the situation that you left behind?" he asked.

The situation he left behind?

"I'm not sure I follow, sir."

The general glanced at the other generals, then at something behind Lucky.

A nurse pushed his way between the generals.

He didn't look at Lucky or the generals. He reached up over Lucky's head.

Lucky realized that he wasn't restrained by the pod restraints. He was just being restrained, period.

"He's telling the truth," said the nurse.

"Bullshit," said a two-star with a hard accent.

The four-star held up his hand.

Lucky'd had enough.

"Can someone spell it out," he said, then as an afterthought, "sirs."

The general looked again at the men standing around Lucky. He nodded his head, and the men made room for a fourth person.

"They are calling it Lucky Lane," said Jiang. "Personally, I think it's a little on the nose, but what can you do?"

Lucky strained his head forward to see her. In shorts and a tank top, she looked even more muscular. Her arms and legs were tree trunks. Lucky was a gym rat, but she put him to shame.

"Jiang," he said. "What the hell—"

"Goddammit, Jiang," exploded a voice from the doorway. Malby strutted into the room. "The less clothes you wear, the more you look like a man."

Jiang sighed. "Dawson dusted off, and I'm stuck with this guy."

Lucky looked up sharply. "Dawson is gone?"

She nodded. "Popsicled up and headed home a few hours ago. Something about seeing his daughter before the end of the universe. Go figure."

"The end of the universe? I thought we took care of that, Rocky."

"Don't look at me."

"Hey," Malby said, glancing around as if he was just noticing where he was. "You're finally thawed."

He held up a large tumbler. "Have a little go-go juice."

Lucky smelled the rocket fuel on his breath and knew what was in the tumbler.

"Thanks, Malby, for making me feel like the mature one."

Malby flashed a grin. "Hey, man, I thought I'd be dead by now. I would be dead by now." He paused, then looked around. "We all would be," he said louder, in the direction of the generals. Either Malby had a death wish or a drinking problem, but either way, he shouldn't be in the same room as three generals.

"Maybe you should just let Jiang—"

"Did you tell him?" Malby asked Jiang. "Did she tell you?" he asked Lucky.

"No!" yelled Lucky. "No one has told me a damn thing!"

His head was starting to hurt, his mind still fuzzy from the freeze.

Malby looked at him with a crooked grin. "There's that temper again."

Jiang cut in. "We are in route to the"—she hesitated, lowering her voice—"Great Corridor."

"Lucky Lane," said Malby conspiratorially.

"Why are we going there?" Lucky said. "Who is going there?"

Malby laughed. "Everybody in the universe is going there."

Suddenly, Lucky felt sick.

"*No way,*" said Rocky.

This was the part where he got loud and drunk and didn't have to apologize for it. He had earned some damned R&R.

"Lucky," said Jiang, resting her hand on his shoulder. "It stayed open."

"What stayed open?" he asked stupidly.

"The hole in the universe!" Malby exclaimed, throwing his arms wide and spilling his drink.

The generals walked out of the room, still talking quietly among themselves.

Lucky looked over at Jiang.

She was nodding. "It didn't close. The Great Corridor."

"Lucky Lane!" slurred Malby.

Jiang ignored him. "And it doesn't look like it's going to."

EPILOGUE

THEY CAME TENTATIVELY AT FIRST.

There was terrible destruction here.

Desolation.

But rumors flew faster than facts or fear.

There was something else here, they whispered.

A lucky accident.

A cosmic mistake.

An ancient power had been released, and a window into another place had been thrown open.

What kind of place?

The rumors would not say.

The reasonable scoffed.

There was nowhere to run from the Da'hune and their endless war.

But rumors need no rest, no destination.

They just fly, growing as they go.

Soon, the rumors were facts.

A barren universe with abundant resources.

A place to start over.

And so they came, ready to try their luck.

And then more followed.
And more still.
The kind and the hateful, the scared and the powerful.
To a pristine new place, far from the war.
Space to find peace at last, surely.
A lucky universe.

TO BE CONTINUED

"IT DIDN'T LOOK anything like you. We altered it. Excessively."

General Artimes scowled. "You saw how he reacted in there."

"It doesn't matter," said Lewis. "The Orton clone served its purpose. We learned a valuable amount in a short period of time."

"We learned that we were being double-crossed," shot back Artimes.

"I beg to differ."

The two generals turned to their superior counterpart, Commandant Apollo.

"It could not have worked out better," he offered.

Lewis and Artimes exchanged glances.

"The plan failed, Saul."

"Spectacularly."

"We gave them everything they asked for—everything—and instead of delivering on the weapons they promised, they were planning to turn everything we gave them against us."

The Commandant shrugged. "We were planning to do the same to them."

All agreed on that front.

"The Emperor won't be amused when he figures out what we are up to," said Lewis.

"And what are we up to, Tim?"

Lewis fell silent.

"Without proof, the Senate won't let the old man act. His hands are tied."

"And this disaster has cleared itself up nicely. We still have the Elites. We have plenty of their weapons. And we don't have *them* to worry about."

"For now."

"For now," agreed Apollo. "We'll deal with that when the time comes."

"I'm the presiding overseer of the Society, Saul. It's easy for you to be so ... positive. They won't come for you first."

Apollo shrugged. "Rightly so."

"What's that supposed to mean?" Lewis shot back bitterly. "The Society has been working with those agents for a hundred years. Your father. My father. Your grandfather. My grandfather. How can you possibly call this my fault?"

"You preside over the Society. This is your responsibility."

"They'll hang you, too."

"They'll hang us all eventually."

Lewis ran his hand through his hair and exhaled deeply. "So how do you suggest I proceed?"

Apollo looked back at the hospital room where Lucky, Jiang and Malby were still talking.

"You start by taking care of the loose ends."

PLEASE LEAVE A REVIEW

Thank you for reading *Lucky Universe!*

If you enjoyed my book, please consider leaving a review on Amazon.

Just a quick star rating and a sentence or two can make a huge difference.

It is critically important to have reviews. You probably weigh reviews highly when making a decision whether to try a new author or rely on an old favorite—I know that I do. Apart from helping to persuade people to give a new writer a shot, reviews help drive sales which, in turn, mean that Amazon takes notice and starts to market on my behalf. And no one markets books better than Amazon.

Best wishes,
Joshua James

A WORD FROM JOSHUA

If you've made it this far, I'm guessing you enjoyed meeting our friend Lucky. (That, or you just have a masochistic need to finish books you dislike!)

If you're looking for more Lucky, then look no further.

The story continues in a series of fast-paced thrillers that take Lucky (and you) all around the universe.

First up, if you haven't picked up the free prequel, LUCKY SHOT (Reader Crew exclusive), I encourage you to do so. In it, we take a trip back in time to meet Lucky when he was just a green private, still trying to find his place in the universe—and trying not to get humiliated by his far-more-accomplished sister.

In LUCKY LEGACY, the direct sequel to the book you just finished, we find Lucky and Co. dealing with the fallout from the opening of the Great Corridor—and racing to stop a conspiracy that could bring the entire Empire to its knees.

In LUCKY EMPIRE, Lucky faces his greatest challenge yet: A ghost from his past that may hold the key to clearing his name—or turn all of mankind upon itself.

You can grab them individually or save by downloading the Box Set (containing all three thrillers, plus Lucky Universe, all in one convenient package).

What are you waiting for? The fun is just starting—once you get Lucky, you won't be able to stop...

GET EXCLUSIVE LUCKY MATERIAL

Building a relationship with my readers is the very best thing about writing. I occasionally send newsletters with details on new releases, special offers, and other bits of news relating to the series I'm writing. If you sign up for the mailing list I'll send you this free Lucky content:

- A free copy of Lucky's prequel adventure, LUCKY SHOT.
- An eyes-only profile of Lucky from an Empire psychologist.

Visit www.LuckyShotBook.com today!

Published by down7media, LLC

Cover art by Tom Edwards (TomEdwardsDesign.com)

Printed in Great Britain
by Amazon

85154131R00174